Big Al the Dream Maker's Emporium of Curiosities,
Oddities, and Strange Things

Big AL the Dream Maker's
EMPORIUM
OF CURIOSITIES ODDITIES AND STRANGE THINGS

ALAN MCGILL

Big Al the Dream Maker's
Emporium of Curiosities, Oddities, and Strange Things
©2024 Alan McGill

All rights reserved. No part of this publication may be reproduced in any form or by any electronic or mechanical means, including information storage and retrieval systems, without permission in writing by the publisher, except by a reviewer who may quote brief passages in a review. For information regarding permissions, contact the publisher at alan.mcgill2020@gmail.com

This book is available at special discounts when purchased in quantity for educational purposes or for use as premiums, promotions, or fundraisers. For inquiries and details, contact the publisher at alan.mcgill2020@gmail.com

Paperback ISBN: 979-8-9899695-6-2
ebook ISBN: 979-8-9899695-5-5

Cover Design by Emily's World of Design
Interior Design by Liz Scheiter
Editing by Anthony Avina

For my wonderful companion, Stormy. Thank you for your friendship and always being there for me.
I miss you

Welcome to the
EMPORIUM

Please close the door.

Mind not the bell, it will cease as you walk the floor.

Fear not the Poliger for she will not bite.

No harm will befall you, if your heart is right.

I am Big Al the Dream Maker, and this is my store.

A place of Mystery and Wonder to its core.

Everything has a price, yet nothing is for sale

Find what you need to pierce the veil.

Hello dear friend.

I see you have found my little shop. As I've already introduced myself to you in rhyme, I shall do so again, with less this time. Sorry, I could not help it. Anyway, as I was saying, I am Big Al the Dream Maker, sole proprietor of The Emporium. (hears a meow) Excuse me, Stormy here would like me to tell you that she helps manage the shop with me.

Back to my introduction. I never know where WE will end up, the store often chooses the most unlikely places. But there is always a purpose to those who enter. I wonder what your purpose is for being here. Well, there will be plenty of time for you to tell me about it later.

For now, let's talk about the stories. Contained within these pages are five shorts of supernatural suspense. Tales too inconceivable for most, yet I ask you to suspend your beliefs, embrace your imagination, and consider the impossible.

Our setting is the small forest town of Marienville, Pennsylvania, gateway to the Allegheny National Forest. The names have been changed to protect the innocent, but the places and stories are very real, I assure you.

So please, take a look around, don't mind Lilly, she won't hurt you. If you have any questions, please let either Stormy or myself know.

FIVE SHORTIES OF SUPERNATURAL SUSPENSE

AND WHERE YOU CAN FIND THEM
You didn't think I was just going to list them like every other book out there, did you?

The Whistling Woods
21

No Time for Murder
47

Eye for Trouble
65

Penny for Your Thoughts
1

The Grinning Man
87

PENNY
FOR YOUR
THOUGHTS

Simon drove through Marienville like he'd done a hundred times before. Work wasn't going well and his mind drifted. He'd taken the back roads partly because it was the most direct route, partly because he loved the forest, but mostly to avoid the law.

He'd narrowly avoided an accident not twenty minutes ago. The hard rain had caused tar beads to surface on the blacktop, making the road slick. The fog had also amassed over the valleys between the dense trees, lowering visibility. All of this and a distracted mind were a bad combination.

A semi-truck climbed the steep hill in front, but the fog prevented Simon from seeing it. He came upon it fast, and there was little he could do. He tapped the brakes, but the tires didn't grip, so he cut the wheel jutting into the passing lane.

He raced to overtake the big truck but wasn't quite there when bright lights blinded him, along with the sound of a horn blaring. Simon turned the wheel sharply to get back onto his side of the road. He fishtailed as the eighteen-wheeler he cut off honked its horn. Simon looked in his rearview mirror and took a deep breath.

Simon's heart was still racing when he pulled to the pumps of the local convenience store. The last thing he needed was an accident with two ounces of cocaine in the car.

The drugs were hidden in a McDonald's bag lying next to him on the seat. He knew the cops, nor anyone else, would ever think to look in it, but if he was in an accident, anything could happen. He locked the bag in the glove box before entering the store.

The lights were on, but there were no customers inside. In fact, there wasn't anybody around. He knew the office was across from the bathroom in the back. Maybe the clerk was in there?

Simon had stopped here several times before to use the restroom. He'd get a peek at the camera monitors if the office door was open. They were useful to see if anyone followed him. The cameras once showed a sheriff's car pulled in to get gas. Simon waited in the store until they left. That was two weeks ago, and he swore it would be the last time, yet here he was again.

Simon walked down the hall, but the office door was closed. He put his ear to it but couldn't hear anything.

"Hello," Simon called but got no reply.

He tried the knob, but the door was locked. Simon tapped on the door and said a bit louder, "HELLO." The response was the same.

Simon walked to the counter in the front, but the store was empty. He really wanted a bottle of water. He didn't have any cash and couldn't use his card without somebody at the register. *Where the hell is the clerk?*

Simon looked outside and noticed there wasn't any traffic either. Route 66 wasn't heavily traveled this time of night, but it usually had some cars. He expected to see the semi coming past, but it never did. He also realized the fog was gone. The night was clear and full of stars.

While he really wanted that drink, Simon wasn't about to steal. He walked to his car and tried the pump, but his card didn't work. Now, his stress returned.

Simon went back inside and checked the office again. He tried the doorknob, only this time, it turned. He gingerly opened the door to poke his head through, "HEY, ANYBODY HERE. I REALLY NEED GAS. I'M NOT SURE I CAN MAKE IT HOME. I'M DAMN NEAR OUT OF...." The office was empty.

Simon didn't have all night; he had to meet his contact before he could go home, and it was getting late. The next town was twenty miles south and not on his way. The extra miles pissed him off, but there wasn't much choice.

Simon hurried back to his car and started down the road. As he was about to pass the main intersection in town, his car began to act funny. "Oh shit. What now?"

The electrical system blinked on and off like it was going to shut down. The radio changed channels as if controlled by an unknown force. The vehicle sputtered and jerked, and then suddenly, everything went back to normal. Simon let out a sigh and kept going.

As he drove through town, there wasn't anyone around, just like the store. None of the homes had lights, yet the streetlamps were on, so the electricity wasn't out. Simon slowed as he passed Ray's Hot Spot at the other end of town. The beer signs were all on, but the parking lot was empty. It was as if the bar was open, but there weren't any customers.

I'm in a hurry, or I'd stop for a drink. He thought.

Simon continued past Ray's as the highway became even darker. That's when he noticed the glow of neon up ahead. Then, the vehicle began to act funny again. The lights flickered, the engine sputtered, but it felt different this time. The fuel gauge showed he was low on gas but wasn't empty yet, so he wasn't out of fuel. This was something else.

The closer he got to the neon lights, the worse the car reacted. "NO, no, no, no, not tonight." He pleaded.

The engine quit, and the lights went out. "DAMN IT. I ain't got time for this." Simon slid the shifter to neutral and drifted off the road into the parking lot. *Where'd that come from?* An illuminated sign on the front of the building read. *Emporium of Curiosities, Oddities, & Strange Things.*

Simon stopped, wondering how he had suddenly found himself in front of this place. He pushed the start button several times, but nothing. "Son of a bitch!" He checked his phone. It was black. "Ah, C'MON. This can't be happening."

He got out of the car and stared at the big neon sign. A heavy breeze rolled leaves and paper across the lot. The glow from the sign illuminated the road for a short distance. Everything was black beyond its reach. The stars of the sky showed the jagged skyline of tall timber.

The parking lot was empty, just like Kwik-Fill and Ray's Hot Spot. Simon shut the car door but had to use the key to lock it, as none of the electronics worked. He looked up and down the highway, but it was desolate.

The neon sign crackled as he got closer. Suddenly, he could see his breath, which was odd because it was the middle of summer. Simon went to the front door, pressing his face to the glass. He could see a light in the back of the little shop. It was above a counter that stretched from wall to wall, with an oversized register in the middle.

He reached for the doorknob and was surprised to hear the latch. He expected it to be locked, but it swung open with ease. A bell above his head rang twice, once when it opened and again when he closed the door behind him.

The sound echoed as if it traveled a great distance. He looked at the counter, which seemed much farther than he saw from outside. From the parking lot, this place looked to be little more than a small candy shop, but inside, it appeared to be huge.

The shop was filled with various things. There were glass cases on both walls that extended all the way down both sides, converging at the counter.

There was taxidermy of all kinds everywhere. Simon's heart nearly stopped when he came face to face with the giant Poliger to his left. It was so lifelike he did a double take. The fur on its head brushed the ceiling as the beast was posed on its hind legs. There was a menacing snarl and outstretched claws, which made it look even more fearsome.

The walls had weird birds, reptiles, and small mammals. They all looked familiar, yet none were species he recognized. They were scattered among the racks of vintage clothes, tools, coins, weapons, carvings, stones, glass bottles, paintings, records, and other strange things. There were old signs of all kinds. Retired doctors, dentists, and other professionals. You name it, it was in here. There wasn't an empty space to be had.

Simon worked his way through the maze of antiquities until he found himself standing before the counter. The oversized cash register was to his right. The buttons were so big that Andre the Giant could operate them. Its dull bronze and stained oak stood out but fit the décor of this odd place.

He looked back at the door, which was small, like it was miles away. Even the Poliger seemed tiny. *How can that be? The store isn't that big?* He thought.

His head turned abruptly when the curtains moved. An unusual man named Al, Big Al, to be precise, peeled the curtains apart while holding onto his hat. He stepped to the counter, taking a sip from his mug. Steam rolled into the air as the smell of ground coffee reached Simon's nose.

Big Al greeted Simon with a warm smile. "May I help you?"

Simon's voice trembled. "My car broke down." Then he showed the man his phone, "And my battery went dead. Any chance I could borrow your cell?"

"Cell?" Big Al asked.

"Yeah, you know…to make a call," Simon answered.

The shopkeeper took another sip. "Never liked them."

"You don't have a cell phone? That's a little Strange." Simon took a long pause to look around. "Um, I've been traveling this road for years. I never noticed your shop before."

"Seems like an odd time to be traveling. Being so late. What's your name, friend?" Big Al asked.

"Me, oh, ah, I'm Simon. You own this place?"

"This shop has been in business for many years. Perhaps you never noticed it because you never needed it before." Big Al's eyes squinted as he watched Simon contemplate what he'd just told him.

"The shop isn't much use to me if you don't have a phone."

"I never said I didn't have a phone. There are other ways to communicate besides a cell phone." Big Al grinned.

Simon's expression lifted. "You have a landline?"

"Of sorts." Big Al walked in the direction of the wall to his left. "Follow me."

Simon looked at Big Al and then back to the counter several times. "How the...?" He never saw Big Al come from behind the counter. And he didn't hear Big Al climbing over it either. Simon squatted to get a better look, but there wasn't a break anywhere. It was one solid piece from wall to wall. *How the hell did this guy get out here?*

"You comin?" Big Al called out. He was about twenty feet away now. *How'd he get that far?* Simon hurried to catch up, but it seemed to take forever. Big Al went to a lighted area and stopped.

"What is that?" Simon asked.

Big Al pulled the handle to open the folding door. "It's called a phone booth. Came all the way from New York City. It's a vintage piece. Not many of these babies around. That you can count on. I guess you're lucky it's here." A light shined inside over an old rotary phone.

Simon leaned in and squinted. "The slot says...2 cents?"

"That's the cost." Big Al could see he didn't understand, "To make a call."

Simon looked even more confused, "I don't have any pennies. I keep them in a jar at home."

The counter right behind the phone booth displayed dozens of coins. Each was encased in white cardboard with a mylar hole to view them. Big Al ran his finger over the glass, searching, until he came to the coins he wanted. "There."

"How much are those?" Simon knew coins in casings like that were usually rare and hard to find. They were items worth more than the stamped value. *I see now. Clever. It's a way to get me to buy some overpriced relic.* He thought.

"You're right. They are rare. But not for sale." Big Al commented. Simon hadn't said what he was thinking out loud. It was like Big Al read his mind. Which, of course, he did. In a way.

"Not for sale?" Simon asked. "I don't mind paying to make a call. I can buy something else if you can give me the coins."

"How? You don't have any cash." Big Al said.

How does he know I don't have cash? Simon's mind raced.

"But you misunderstand, friend; nothing is for sale in here." Big Al turned to face Simon, whose first instinct was fear. "You won't need that friend. You're in no danger in this shop."

Simon didn't realize his hand slid under his coat. His fingers curled around the handle of his gun. He looked down embarrassed, loosened the grip, and relaxed.

Big Al stretched his arm around the back of the counter and retrieved two of the pennies. He extended them to Simon. "Barter only."

Simon was confused. "I don't have anything to trade."

"We all have something of value." Still dangling the two coins, Big Al extended his other arm to showcase the store, "One's junk is another's treasure."

"The only thing I have is my cell phone, and it doesn't work. Otherwise, I wouldn't be here. And my, well..." Simon shuffled.

"I don't want your gun, Simon. I have plenty of those." Big Al pointed at the wall where a dozen pistols were prominently displayed.

"Are those loaded?" Simon hadn't noticed them before.

A devious smile formed over Big Al's face. "Not much use otherwise." The smile faded as he took a step toward Simon. Big Al held the pennies in the palm of his hand. His brim had cast a shadow over his face, which amplified the twinkle in his eye. "These are irreplaceable. You'd need something a little more valuable than a Glock 27. "

"If you're trying to suggest I trade my soul, that's a bit much. Even if I was a believer, making a phone call seems like a heavy price." Simon's sarcasm helped overcome his fear.

"Depends on the call, wouldn't you say? Listen, friend, the worth of anything is what someone else is willing to pay. Nothing more." Big Al's smile returned. "But no, I don't want your soul." He grew impatient with Simon. "Well, do you want to make the phone call? Or not?"

"Yes, but like I said, I don't have anything."

"What about the item in your glove box?" Big Al sneered.

The fear returned. "How do you know what's in my glovebox?" How could this guy have known what he'd done? That happened hours ago, two counties over, and nobody saw anything.

"Are you going to call the sheriff?" Beads of sweat formed on Simon's brow.

Big Al chuckled. "Wolfgang. No. He'll lock you up for sure. But you shouldn't worry about that right now. You should decide who you're going to call. You only get one. The booth only takes pennies, and I only have enough for one call." Big Al stepped into the light so Simon could see his face under the brim of his hat. "You know what's coming, don't you?"

"But I need it." Simon pleaded.

"Tell you what, friend, you seem like a nice kid. Let's call it a trade for your services." Big Al suggested.

Simon's brow furled. "Services?"

"Yes. I'll give you the coins. Someday, I'll ask you for a favor. You will do it." Big Al was stoic. His expression was deadly serious.

Simon took a moment to think about everything. He could suddenly hear the clock on the wall as time ticked with an echo. He nodded, taking the coins from the extended palm of Big Al.

He sat in the booth and closed the door. Once the latch clicked, Simon removed the pennies from their casings and slid them into the slot. He listened as they rattled their way through the machine. Once seated, he picked up the receiver and placed it to his ear. "How the… hell does this work?" Big Al was standing outside, making a circle with his index finger.

Simon got the idea. He'd never used a rotary phone. Hell, he'd never even seen one in real life. The rotation mesmerized him as he dialed each number. After the last one, the phone rang. It continued to ring several times, but nobody answered. Simon placed the earpiece back on the receiver. Dejected.

It startled him when the phone dumped the pennies into the return slot, but a glimmer of hope returned. Simon repeated the process. Again, it just rang and rang. He retrieved the pennies again and opened the door. "Nobody answered."

"Are you sure you dialed the correct number?" Big Al asked.

"Yes, I know the number. Somebody should have been there, but it just rang." Simon extended the pennies to Big Al. "Here, I guess I didn't need them after all."

"Sorry, my friend. A deal's a deal. You sealed it the moment you ran them through the phone. I'm afraid you still owe me a favor."

"What? The deal was for a call. I just told you nobody answered. Besides, there wasn't anything special about them. They're just ordinary pennies. Worth two…" Simon snipped.

Before Simon could say anything else, Big Al had him by the throat and slammed against the wall. His forearm was under Simon's chin lifting him off the ground while his other hand clenched a fistful of hair. He yanked Simon's head to the side, which caused tears to well in the young man's eyes.

Big Al leaned in close. His eyes glowed red with anger. Simon could feel Big Al's silver whiskers move as his tone was full of malice. "The deal was for the pennies, so you could make a call. I never said they were worth anything other than to you. You owe me a favor, and you're going to do it. Now, I suggest you try again. I would make sure you make the right call. Once it goes through, you're out of options."

Big Al let go, and Simon fell to the floor. He reached for the gun in his anger, but it was gone!

"Looking for this?" Big Al held up the pistol with two fingers with a mean scowl on his face, "Make your call."

Simon slowly climbed back into the phone booth. He carefully put the pennies into the slot. He was about to dial the same number when Big Al spoke. "Make a good decision, Simon."

Simon hesitated, lifted the receiver, then dialed. It rang two times before he heard a soft, sweet female voice. "Hello."

Simon's eyes closed tight when he heard the sound. He could barely speak but managed to say, "Honey?"

"Simon, is that you?" His wife asked.

"Yes. I'm running a little late, but I'll be home soon." A tear rolled down his cheek.

"Where are you?" she asked with concern. "Whatever you're doing, Simon, don't. Just come home."

He wiped the tear away and steeled himself, "But we need the money."

"Your child needs a father. We'll be okay. Please, Simon, just come home." Her voice was shaky this time, sinking his heart.

"I love you, Leese." Simon hung up the phone before she could respond. He placed his forehead on the receiver. *Please, God, forgive me.* His silent prayer was interrupted by the sound of a truck engine outside. Gravel spewed into the building as the vehicle came to a skidding stop.

Big Al moved to the storefront for a better look. Simon barely noticed they were now close to the front window. "I need my gun. I can't trade it. I'll do whatever you ask, like we agreed." Simon pleaded. "Please, mister. I got a kid on the way."

"You should have thought about that before you went for your gun." Big Al sneered.

"I'll owe you two favors. Whatever you want. Please." Simon begged. "I ain't got nothing else.

Big Al never took his eyes off the truck outside as he responded. "You've got the glove box." Big Al turned to Simon. "Make a good decision."

Simon's eyes got big. His mouth was dry as he spoke, "I don't even want the glovebox anymore, but I can't let anyone else get hurt." Simon was trembling. "I'm sorry I got you into this, mister. But this is my problem, not yours."

Big Al threw the pistol back to Simon. "Do you want my help?"

Simon could see the shadows as figures crossed the headlights outside. They were coming. "You can have the glovebox," he responded.

Big Al smiled, tipped his hat, and said, "Stay inside, friend. Nothing will harm you in here."

"Wait. If you're going out there, take this." Simon said, extending the gun to Big Al.

Big Al tilted his head, "Don't you realize, Simon, that won't solve your problems." The bell above the door chimed twice, once when Big Al opened the door, and a second time when he closed it.

It was quiet at first. Then, the wind increased. The sound grew more intense as the seconds passed. By the time Simon reached the window to look outside, the wind blew furiously. The combination of dust and darkness prevented him from seeing much. The trucks' headlights flickered behind the haze as the big vehicle rocked back and forth.

Then he heard the screams. A deep feeling of dread came over Simon, and he retreated to the phone booth. He peered from behind it as terror filled his body.

Then he heard a ferocious sound. Several roars filled the area, along with the sound of a terrible battle right outside the front door.

Men cried out in agony. Everything went silent for a few seconds before a thundering BOOM! The impact was so powerful that everything shook inside the store.

Simon jumped as a bloody hand slapped against the window. The fingers slid down, leaving a streak of blood behind. Then he heard the frantic pleading behind the swirling wind, "Help us! Please NO, NO, NO, AHHHH."

Everything went quiet again. Seconds passed before he heard tires spin, sending gravel into the building. He couldn't believe the glass didn't break. Then, there was a loud screech as tires hit the pavement.

He could hear the engine getting farther and farther away until there was nothing. GONG, GONG, GONG. A grandfather clock standing against the far wall sounded off. Simon sighed but was startled again when the phone rang.

Simon stretched into the booth to grab the receiver. He looked around nervously as he picked it up. "He-Hello." He answered.

"You can go now, Simon." It was Big Al. "Don't forget our deal."

"What happened to them?" Simon asked.

"They made…poor decisions. But you needn't worry about them anymore, dear friend." Big Al stated.

"Did you, did you kill them?" Simon's voice vibrated with fear.

"You made poor decisions tonight too, Simon. But you redeemed yourself. Go home to Lisa. She needs you."

"But my car. It won't start." Simon stated.

"Try it again." The line clicked before it went dead. Simon looked at the handset, not sure what to think.

It was a long walk to the front door. He looked back before reaching for the knob. The phone booth was far off in the distance. The counter was even farther.

Simon gripped the gun tightly. He looked at the fearsome Poliger before twisting the knob to go out. Its facial expression changed.

It wasn't gruesome like before. *Almost looks like it's smiling now.* He thought. The bell rang as he left and again when he closed the door behind him.

He stepped off the porch gingerly. The wind had stopped; everything was still. The blood on the window was gone, and there was no body under it or any others in the parking lot. The truck was also gone and there was no sign of Big Al.

The area seemed darker than before, as the only light came from the neon sign. It flickered as he walked to his car. Simon fumbled with the keys to unlock the door, and the moment it was open, the neon went out.

Simon didn't waste any time. He shut the door and pushed the start. The engine roared, and lights came on. He thrust the shifter into drive and floored the gas. The wheels spun, sending gravel and dust out the back, and the tires chirped when they made contact with the highway.

As he sped away, his eyes went to the glovebox. Big Al said he wanted the glovebox, but the car was locked, and Simon had the key.

That's when he saw the red and blue flashing lights in his review mirror. Panic set in, and he considered running. But knew he'd be caught. His eyes drifted to the glovebox again. If the cops looked in there, he'd go to jail for a long time.

Suddenly, Big Al's voice. *Make a good decision, Simon.* Was that in his mind? Or did he hear it?

Simon trembled as he pulled the car to the side of the road and lowered the window.

"Where ya off to in such a hurry, son?" the deputy asked. "Do me a favor and shut the engine off, will ya?"

"I, I was just going home, sheriff," Simon answered.

"Let me see your license, registration, and proof of insurance."

Simon's heart plummeted. A lump formed in his throat, and he knew the moment he opened the glovebox, the deputy would see the

McDonald's bag. If it were lying on the floor or sitting on the seat, it was no big deal, but stuffed into a glovebox? His hands shook as he leaned across the seat and turned the latch.

The deputy could smell the fear on Simon. His hand moved to grip his pistol while his other hand kept a light on the glove box. As the lid fell, revealing the inside, Simon blinked in disbelief, took a deep breath, and closed his eyes.

Meanwhile, Big Al could see the sheriff car's red and blue lights from inside the Emporium. He took a sip of coffee before grabbing the McDonald's bag from the counter. With a pursed smile, he disappeared into the back.

Simon waited patiently for the deputy with a sigh of relief.

"I'm going to give you a warning. There ain't any houses, but don't give you the right to tear up a driveway. Spinnin tires can throw gravel and do some damage. Since I couldn't see any, I'm not gonna cite you. Just don't do it again." The deputy stated.

"Sorry, officer, I just pulled into the store there. Had a bit of car trouble."

"Store?" the deputy asked. "What store, son? You mean the camp? Casey's Corner is a local landmark but not a…store."

Simon turned his head to see the Emporium was gone. A streetlamp on the corner shined over a small block camp sitting on the corner lot.

"Wait, there was a store called the Empor…" Simon didn't bother to finish the sentence.

"You ain't been drinkin', have you?" The deputy asked.

"No, sir. Just trying to get home to my wife and unborn son." Simon answered.

"Alright. Well, be careful. Lots of deer." The deputy returned to his car, turned off the emergency lights, and drove away.

Simon sat in the dark for a moment. He looked up at the stars and thought about Lisa and his unborn son. He pushed the start button, heard the engine fire, and slowly pulled away.

What did you think? Was Simon a good guy? I'd say Big Al not only saved his life but kept him from years in prison too. I wonder if the detective in my new sci-fi thriller *Bumper City* would have arrested Simon?

If you want to know the answer to that question, I guess you'll just have to read the book and decide for yourself. *Bumper City* is available just about anywhere books are sold.

Sci-fi Detective Thriller

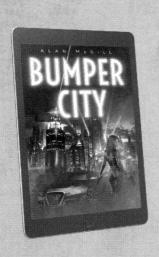
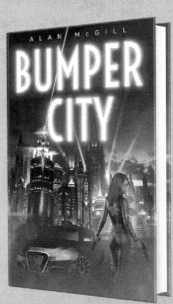

SUCKS YOU IN!

I love this book and how it sucks you in from the very beginning. The twists and turns throughout the book keep you guessing and wondering who the bad guy really is. Just when you think you have it figured out, another twist in the plot emerges, sending you back to square one. This is a definite poolside summer read.

**AND NOW,
ON WITH
OUR SHOW!**

THE WHISTLING WOODS

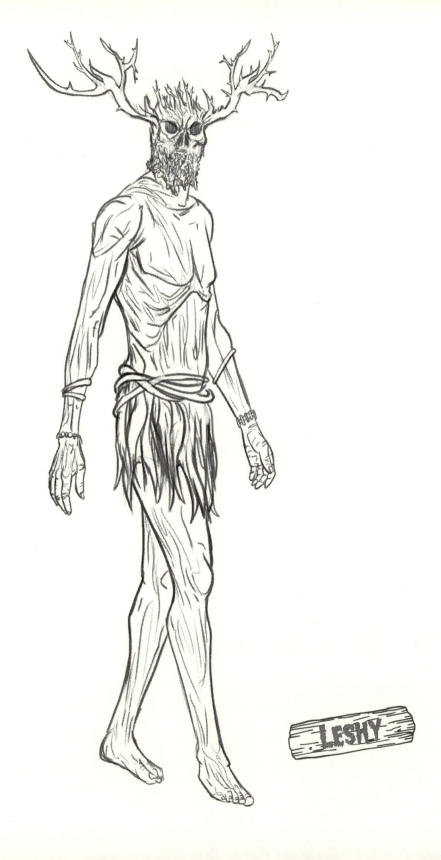

Marion and Dean were a young couple living an unassuming life in Erie, Pennsylvania. But their relationship was a troubled one. They'd met in college. Dean played tight end for the Warren Dragons, earning him a scholarship at Mercyhurst University. Marion excelled at cross-country and swimming at McDowell High School, but injuries prevented her from obtaining an athletic scholarship.

Dean was an avid outdoorsman who enjoyed hunting and fishing. Marion was a city girl but loved the outdoors. She spent her free time at places like Presque Isle State Park. They seemed like a match made in heaven, that is until Dean discovered Marion had cheated on him.

Despite the infidelity, Dean loved Marion, and she loved him. Dean was determined to make it work. They'd planned a long weekend together in the Allegheny National Forest. The two intended to work on their relationship by hiking on some trails near the small town of Marienville.

The plan was to leave Friday after class, drive to a campsite, and hit the first trail before sunset. The next day, the two would rise early and hike the next trail. The alone time would allow them to talk and, hopefully, repair the damage already done.

Dean's class finished right after lunch. He'd asked Marion to prepare sandwiches and other food for their excursion. He packed the car the night before as they both wanted everything ready so they could leave without delay.

"Hey Babe, can you grab me a water?" The long drive made Dean thirsty.

Marion opened the cooler behind his seat, "Dean, is this all the water you brought?" She handed him the bottle and said, "You're going to have to stop at the Kwik Fil. I can't drink this."

"Sorry, Mare, it's all they had." Dean was determined to stay positive.

"It's okay. I'll get some at the store." Marion said.

It was almost evening when Dean pulled into the Kwik-Fill outside of Marienville. The moon was visible in the blue sky as they parked. Marion ran inside while he pumped gas.

Marion picked up a case of the water she preferred and a Three Musketeers Bar for Dean. "That'll be $6.87," the clerk said. Marion tapped the card reader with her Visa. "Are you guys going camping?" the clerk asked.

Marion smiled. "Yeah." Suddenly, the card reader started to beep. "I'm sorry, your card's been declined," the clerk stated. "You could try the chip."

Marion inserted the card, but the result was the same. "I'm not sure what's wrong. I'll be right back." She was about to open the door when she heard an angry Dean, "SON OF A BITCH."

The gas pump handle hadn't clicked, and a burst of fuel splashed over Dean's pant leg. Marion hurried to him but had to cover her mouth from laughing when she saw. He'd peeled off his pants and was standing in his underwear.

"You okay?" Marion snickered. Dean was red-faced, "Yeah, I'm good, thanks for asking." He sneered, grabbing a pair of shorts from the back seat. Then she noticed his hand. "Oh my God. You're bleeding."

"When I grabbed the pump, it pinched my thumb. There's a bandage in the first aid kit." Dean said.

As Marion reached for the glovebox, Dean stopped her. "I'm good I said. I'll get it." Dean was snippy. "What did you need?" He asked, pushing past her to retrieve the first aid kit.

"The card you gave me isn't working. Do you have another?" She asked.

Dean leaned into the front of the car and pulled a $20 bill from his wallet. "Nice legs." Marion joked, trying to lighten the mood. She turned quickly but tripped over the pump hose. She didn't fall, but the clerk saw her stumble on the camera monitor.

She came through the door a little embarrassed. "Everything all right out there, miss?" The clerk asked. "Seems like you two are having a day."

"A little gas spilled. Nothing to worry about." After paying for the water and the candy bar, Marion rushed back to the car.

Dean had just finished bandaging his finger. "I'm sorry I snapped."

"It's okay." Marion looked around, "Where are your pants?" Dean pointed to the area behind her seat. "I put them in one of the garbage bags. We can wash them later." Marion handed Dean the candy bar and kissed his cheek.

As he drove, Marion laid her head on the headrest. The tension between them was palpable. The incident at the gas station didn't help. Every little hiccup seemed like a big deal, even if it wasn't.

"You okay?" He asked. "We don't have to hike right now if you aren't up to it. We can go to the campground and relax."

"No, no, I'm fine. It's probably the dry air, allergies, or something. It'll pass once we get moving." She responded. "How about you? You're the one with the injured finger."

"I'm fine. It throbs a little, but it's fine." Dean replied.

Dean drove straight to the Buzzard Swamp trailhead. Two cars were parked in the lot, empty, their owners undoubtedly somewhere on the trail. Dean parked at the far end, away from them.

As he got everything ready, Marion tried to open the glovebox, but it was locked. "Dean, I need the keys."

He tossed them to her, and when she opened the glovebox, she yelled, "Dean, WHAT THE FUCK?"

"I was at the range yesterday and didn't have time to drive back to my parents' house. I didn't want to leave it in the apartment. It's safely locked in there." He responded.

"I hate these things." Marion was huffy but decided to let it go. With two fingers, she moved the pistol out of the way to grab a box of tissues.

Dean retrieved the small pack from the backseat and went through it, making sure everything was there. Marion was already on the trail as he lagged behind. "C'mon, Dean, let's go." She yelled impatiently. When Dean shut the car door, she pressed the key fob to lock it.

Dean pulled the straps tight and hustled to catch her. Marion slowed, and once they were together, she picked up the pace. They walked a little while before coming to a trail that branched in another direction. "There's a lot of trails in here," she commented.

"Yeah, we can hit those tomorrow," Dean said.

"You don't want to try some now?" Marion asked. "Let's at least go on the Songbird Sojourn."

"Most of the songbirds are active in the morning. Wouldn't you rather wait until tomorrow?" He asked.

"Why wait? Let's just check it out." Marion didn't give him a chance to respond; she just marched ahead.

They walked less than a quarter mile before hearing birdsong. "Is that a cat?" Marion asked.

"No, it's a Gray Catbird. A member of the Mockingbird family." Dean said proudly.

Marion didn't expect Dean to know anything about birds. "I'm impressed, big guy. I didn't realize you liked songbirds."

Dean laughed and pointed to a post near the trail. "It's on the sign."

Marion slapped his arm playfully. Both could feel the tension starting to lift. This was the first time since Marion cheated, they felt like their old selves. *Maybe he can forgive me.* Marion thought. And Dean thought, *we'll see.*

A slight breeze rustled through the trees, but there was little birdsong. The farther down the trail, the fewer birds they could hear. The two were having such a good time that they barely noticed the sun was beginning to set. The forest appeared darker, and the temperature began to drop.

Marion became chilly. She stopped to grab a sweater from Dean's backpack, but he was standing several yards back eating one of the sandwiches she'd prepared.

He took a couple of bites and then bent over like he was going to be sick. "Dean?" She called as he took a knee.

He stood up straight and looked at her, then turned to the woods. "Babe?" She called, taking a few steps closer. He didn't answer but continued to stare at the woods. "Babe? I need my sweater." But Dean wasn't responding, so Marion hurried toward him, "Babe? Babe? Wha…What are you looking at?"

Dean said nothing; he just stared in a trance-like state. He jumped when she touched his elbow. "Ahh!"

Marion laughed nervously, "Babe, it's just me? You, you okay? You sick?"

Dean gave a short, hesitating laugh. He looked at her sheepishly and then returned his gaze to the forest. "Did you hear that?"

"Hear what?" She looked in the direction he was, but Marion didn't know what he was talking about.

They both stood motionless. There were no sounds, birds, or rustling of leaves on the trees; everything was still. Dean opened his mouth to speak when a low whistle came through the trees. It was short and barely audible, but it was there.

Dean turned to Marion, "You hear it?" he asked.

Marion nodded slowly. "What is that?"

She expected him to name some bird, but he didn't respond. His expression was blank like before. He took two small steps off the trail when she whispered. "Dean! Where are you going?"

Then, out of nowhere, he ran! Dean bolted up the small hill in the direction of the whistle. "DEAN! DEAN! WHERE ARE YOU GOING?" Marion yelled.

Seconds later, he disappeared over the hill into the dark woods. She could hear the stomping of his feet over leaves and the breaking of sticks, but she couldn't see him. She heard him getting farther and farther away until the last drop of sunlight disappeared from the sky. Then she couldn't hear anything, and Dean was completely gone!

"DEAN!" Marion yelled. "DEEEEAAAN!" She yelled again. There was no sound, no reply.

Then, quietly, she heard it again, the weird low whistle as if calling to her now.

Marion's heart started to pound. Her breath increased. Thoughts raced as she imagined terrible things. What should she do? She couldn't leave him, but she was afraid.

Then, the whistle called to her again. Was her mind playing tricks? Now, she could hear her name in the tune. It seemed to be luring her into the forest. Every fiber in her being told her to run. But how could she leave Dean? It was so dark now, could she even find him?

She thought of calling for help, but her phone was in the backpack. And the backpack was on Dean's back. Then she remembered she had the car keys. He'd tossed them to her so she could get a tissue.

She knew what to do. Marion ran as fast as she could. Her feet pounded the dirt and splashed in puddles until she reached the trailhead. As Marion entered the parking lot, a car was leaving. She tried to get the driver's attention by calling out and waving her arms, but the driver didn't stop.

She raced to her car, used the key fob to unlock the doors, got in, and pushed the ignition button. It just clicked. Frantic, she tried again, but nothing. She pressed the center of the steering wheel, hoping to blare the horn, but there was no sound. In desperation, she hit the emergency SoS button on the roof panel. Again, nothing.

Marion's head collapsed on the steering wheel. More bad thoughts. Panic. She began to sob. Then, as if on cue, a light-filled her car. Across the road, a neon sign glowed with the letters *EMPORIUM Curiosities, Oddities, and Strange Things.*

She wiped away the tears and got out of the car. She hadn't noticed the little store when they pulled in, yet here it was, right across the road. There was another, smaller, neon sign in the window which read, *OPEN*.

Marion ran across the road, bursting through the front door. She gasped at the Poliger looming over her as she entered. She did not expect to see such weird taxidermy when she came through the door. The chime of a bell overhead distracted her from the giant stuffed beast. Its giant outstretched claws and oversized fangs were a scary and unwelcome sight.

A light at the back of the store drew her attention. She could see an antique radio sitting on the counter. Marion quickly filtered past the racks of vintage clothes and display cases. She stopped briefly to eye an antique phone booth halfway to the back counter. Then she heard the voice of a man. "May I help you miss?" He was standing off to the side behind the counter. His white goatee seemed to glow as his hat cast a shadow over his eyes.

Marion rushed toward him. The radio on the counter became louder the closer she got. "Please, please, I need help," she said frantically. "My boyfriend…he wandered off into the woods. I can't find him. I need to call the police."

"Don't you have a phone, young miss?" Big Al asked.

"My boyfriend has it." She replied.

"Why does your boyfriend have your phone?" His inquiry was taking time, and Marion's frustration grew. "It was in our backpack." Marion paused. "Please. I don't have time for this. Can you just call the police?"

"I don't have a telephone. Other than the antique phone booth you saw a few moments ago. Tell me what happened? Perhaps I can help." Big Al tried to reassure her in a calm, collected voice.

Marion took a breath, tried to steady her shaky hands, then began to describe what took place. When she got to the part about the strange whistle, Big Al's interest was piqued. "Did you say a whistle?"

"Yes," Marion replied.

He walked to a bookshelf at the end of the counter. He reached for a scroll wedged between some leather-bound titles among the hundreds of books.

Big Al pointed to the scroll's heading, *LESHY*. He walked back to Marion and rolled out the document before her. "There are all kinds of…strange things in this world, especially this forest. You said your boyfriend, an experienced outdoorsman, liked hunting and fishing?" Big Al thought for a moment before speaking again. "Of course, it could be something else. Lots of creatures in the forest. Alps, Witches, Bigfoot, but Leshy guards the forest. You said…" Big Al paused; Marion jumped in, "Dean."

Big Al smiled, "Perhaps your Dean insulted the Leshy at some point. Or did something against the forest."

"Wha? No. Please, mister. I don't believe in this shi… I just need a phone," Marion pleaded.

"How, then do you explain your boyfriend's erratic behavior? Or the strange whistle?" Big Al said before the radio got louder. A series of beeps ensued, followed by the announcer, *"We interrupt this story for breaking news. A man is feared dead after going missing near Buzzard Swamp outside of Marienville. Police are looking for the man's companion in connection with his disappearance. It is believed this may have been the result of foul play, and this woman is wanted for questioning."*

"WHAT?" Marion yelled.

Big Al placed a finger over his lips. "Shhhh"

Marion's eyes got more prominent as the announcer continued.

"The couple was seen leaving the Kwik-Fill gas station after what appeared to be a domestic altercation. A clerk at the station recalled seeing the woman being thrown to the ground. He said when she returned to the store, he noticed blood on her shirt. Police believe this may be a possible motive. The woman is described as tall, muscular, in her early twenties, with long blond hair. The couple was in a white Subaru Outback with Pennsylvania registration. Anyone with information, please contact the Forest County Sheriff's Office or the Pennsylvania State Police."

"WHAT? HE DIDN'T THROW ME TO THE GROUND. I TRIPPED OVER THE HOSE. AND THE BLOOD WAS DEAN'S." Marion screamed at the radio.

Big Al moved his head slightly to the side, making her even more nervous. "Wait, wait, wait, wait. Dean cut himself on the pump's handle. He got gas all over himself. Some of his blood must have gotten on my shirt." Marion paused, "Oh no. His pants had blood and gas on them. They're in the back of my car!"

Marion's heartbeat increased as her chest moved up and down. "I didn't hurt him; I love him."

"If you call the police, they will arrest you." Big Al said.

"Arrest me? For what?" Marion gasped.

"For killing your boyfriend." He responded.

"ME? What are you talking about? I didn't kill him. I already told you," She started to explain again.

Big Al put his hand up, "I know that. And you know that. But do you think the police will? They'll look in your car and find the pants with the blood and…what else?" Big Al said.

"The gun," Marion muttered.

"What will they think then?" Big Al asked. "Was it recently fired?"

Her heart fell into her stomach. "It's Dean's gun. He went shooting yesterday. He locked it in the glovebox to keep it safe." Marion's lip quivered. "I moved it to get some tissues."

"So, your prints are on it?" Big Al remarked. "I think you'd better find Dean before the police find his gun in your car with your prints. That, along with his bloody clothes..."

"I don't even know where he is," Marion responded.

"I'd say you better find him too. You need to go back to where he disappeared. Start there." Big Al responded. "If it is a *LESHY*, you'll need something to see it with, that and a bottle of Vodka."

"Vodka?" Marion asked.

"According to the scroll." Big Al pointed to a paragraph halfway down the page. *"LESHY* often partake of vodka at local taverns disguised as a human."

"Do you have any vodka?" Marion asked.

"No. But you also need something like, well…" He walked to the bookshelf and pulled down an old book, *Father Daniel's Compendium of the Undead*. He leafed through the book until he reached a drawing that depicted a pair of glasses. The page's title was *Glasses of Revelation*, followed by a description of the object. "…something like these."

"Do you have a pair of those?" Marion asked, looking at all the antiques in his store.

"According to the author, there is only one in existence. However, I have a special pair of glasses infused with Blue Sapphire. Perhaps that is what they are." Big Al walked to the center of the counter. A section under the glass contained various eyeglasses. He scanned the trays before pointing to a singular pair. "These." He pulled the glasses from the case and placed them on a cloth atop the counter before her.

Marion picked up the spectacles, which appeared ordinary except for the blue tint of the lenses. She was about to put them on when Big Al stopped her. "You cannot wear those in here."

"Why?" Marion asked.

"Trust me, only use them outside. And sparingly. The magic from the gems is weak, if there is any magic at all. You may only get one or two uses." He explained.

"How much?" Marion reached for Dean's credit card, which was still in her pocket, but Big Al stopped her.

"I'm afraid they are not for sale." Big Al said. "These are priceless. They might very well be the last ones."

"Isn't this a store?" Marion asked. "If they aren't for sale, why are they in your case? Why did you show them to me?"

"Nothing is for sale in here." Big Al paused. "Barter only."

The hair on the back of Marion's neck stood on end. "You mean a deal? What kind of deal?"

"Depends on our agreement. But whatever arrangement we come to; you will owe me. Someday, could be tomorrow, could be ten years from now, I will ask you to do something." Seeing the tension on her face, Big Al smiled. This was not the warm, comforting smile of before, but rather something sinister. "Don't worry, it won't be anything sexual." Then his mouth returned to normal as the tone of his voice changed. "But whatever I ask of you, you WILL do it."

A lump formed in her throat, and she swallowed hard. Marion nodded slowly. "You said I needed vodka, too. But you don't have any?"

"Yes. We need vodka." Big Al responded.

"We?" Marion asked.

Big Al's head tilted, and his eyes sparkled. "Do we have a deal?"

Marion swallowed again. "What are we agreeing to?"

"Use of the glasses to find your boyfriend. Vodka to convince the *LESHY* to let him go." Big Al stated.

Although Marion didn't believe any of this, she was desperate, and nodded.

"I need to hear you say it." Big Al stated crossly.

"O-Okay." Her answer was soft and reluctant but genuine. "I agree to your terms. Just help me find Dean."

Satisfied, he reached for the rotary phone beside the oversized cash register. Marion watched as he dialed. She'd never seen a phone like that before. She could hear a man's voice answer before Big Al spoke. "You know who this is? Come to the Emporium, I have a job for you. Bring a bottle of Vodka. And not the cheap shit. Something…expensive." Big Al's eyes met Marion's as he spoke into the receiver one last time before hanging up. "Uh? Yes, right now."

"Who was that?" Marion asked.

"Someone like you. Someone in need of a favor long ago." Big Al responded.

Marion jumped as a large grey cat leaped onto the counter. Then she realized Big Al was no longer behind the counter. He was standing next to her, petting the cat. "Watch the counter until I get back, Stormy." The gray Manx reached out with a paw, its claws softly touching his forearm.

"What's that? Ah yes, thank you, Stormy." Big Al responded with a scratch under the cat's chin. Then he picked up the spectacles from the counter and slipped them into his vest pocket.

"Where are you going?" Marion asked.

"I'm going to talk to the cops. Wait here." Big Al said. Marion followed Big Al to the front of the store. Her eyes bugged out when she saw the flashing lights across the road.

"How'd the cops get here? Who called them?" She exclaimed.

"How, indeed?" Big Al smirked as he pulled the front door open. The bell above chimed. It rang again as he closed the door.

She watched him walk across the parking lot, and then a singular thought persisted in her mind: *How did he get across this giant room so fast?*

Night consumed the area. Everything was dark except the trailhead parking area. Big Al's black hat cast a shadow over his face, even below the flashing lights. When he pointed in her direction, Marion gasped. There were two red eyes beneath the brim!

Marion backed away, then composed herself, then went outside. The doors bell chimed as she shut it behind her. Big Al stood beside the cruiser as two sheriff's deputies marched across the road. Her eyes looked past them at Big Al. Below the red eyes, she saw a big white smile.

The deputies were now standing in front of her. "Are you Marion?"

"Ye...yes." She replied.

"Gonna need you to come with us, ma'am. We've got some questions we'd like to ask you."

"O...okay." Marion took a few steps forward, and the moment she was within reach, a deputy spun her around. Before she could react, the second deputy placed her in handcuffs. "Wait. Wait. I didn't do anything! Why are you arresting me?"

"You're under arrest for suspicion of murder."

Big Al was heading down the trail before the deputies took Marion to the parking lot. A tall, skinny man named Thomas was beside him. Thomas looked back to see Marion being shoved in the back of a sheriff's car.

"You bring the vodka?" Big Al asked.

"Right here." The man handed Big Al a fifth of Kettle One.

Big Al was pleased. "Good choice."

"Is that it? Can I go?" The man asked.

"Hardly, Thomas. That's just part of what you owe. You're with me tonight." Big Al answered.

"But..." the man started to object; Big Al cut him off. "It was the vodka and your assistance. Then, your favor is repaid. You don't honestly think what I did for you was only worth a bottle of vodka, do you?" The man, Thomas, lowered his eyes. Embarrassed, maybe ashamed, he couldn't look up. He nodded reluctantly.

Big Al resumed his walk into the dark trail. As the two men continued to walk, Big Al reached into his satchel and retrieved an orb. He raised the object, muttering, "fiat lux." Before the last syllable was spoken, it was as if a switch had been thrown. The orb suddenly emitted a bright light. The intensity of the glow revealed the trail before them.

The two men walked a good mile before coming to the spot where Marion last saw Dean. The forest was noticeably quiet. There were no crickets, night birds, or wind to rustle leaves; it was silent.

Thomas was about to speak when they heard it. Past the trees and over the small hill, there was the sound of a faint whistle. "Trees, right?" Thomas asked nervously.

"It's deliberate. Stops, starts, rhymes. You think the wind does that?" Big Al asked.

"What then?" Thomas was so nervous his lips stuck together.

"Something wicked." Big Al said with a devious smile.

Big Al stepped off the path; leaves crunched beneath his boot. A second step and a twig cracked. Thomas was about to follow when Big Al put out his hand. "You stay here and wait."

"Wait for what?" Thomas asked.

"For something…unexpected." Big Al replied. He turned with a big smile. The whites of his teeth showed brightly under the brim of his hat. "Don't worry, Thomas. I still need you to fulfill the terms of our agreement. You have but one more task to perform."

Goosebumps filled Thomas' arms. Big Al's grin was wide, and his eyes shined. "You'll be alright. Just wait here."

"Then we are square." Thomas was shaking.

"Do this last part, and you will be relieved of your obligation." Big Al smirked.

"What? What am I supposed to do?" Thomas was more frantic this time.

"You'll see." And with that, Big Al tossed him the lighted orb, and disappeared between the dark trees.

Thomas held the orb tightly. He'd thrust the orb toward the sound each time he heard a noise. Beads of sweat ran down his temple. His eyes darted everywhere.

The whistle stopped when Big Al disappeared over the small hill. The forest became quiet again. Then suddenly, a loud boom! The ground trembled. Explosion? Tree fall? The orb's light didn't go far enough. He couldn't even see the hilltop that lay ahead.

Then he heard the worst sound of all. Some type of roar. It blasted from beyond that knob of a hill. This was followed by several loud thumps as if something big were fighting. The raucous continued for several seconds, although it seemed longer to Thomas. Then, another loud roar. Something like a lion or bear. Hell, Thomas even thought it was Godzilla. It was definitely some kind of animal, to be sure, but he didn't know what.

The fear swelled. His thoughts menaced. He was about to run when he heard a faint call for help. A man's voice was getting more robust and louder. Was it Big Al?

As the voice drew closer, he knew it wasn't Big Al. He heard the crunching of leaves and cracking of sticks not far off. Then he noticed the figure of a man staggering from tree to tree, stumbling as he went. The man grasped each tree as if he couldn't stand alone.

Before Thomas realized it, the man was a few feet away. The man fell on his back atop a pile of leaves. Thomas ran over to him, moved to the orb, and looked around. The light reflected off trees, casting shadows. The ground was covered in leaves, sticks, and moss. It was also covered in blood.

"Are you, are you okay? Buddy, are you okay?" Thomas asked.

The man's eyes began to blink as he returned to consciousness. He looked up at Thomas with bewilderment. He nodded yes before asking, "What hap..happened?"

"Are you Dean?" Thomas asked.

The man nodded yes.

"Everyone is looking for you, man," Thomas said. "Where's Big Al? Did you see him?"

"Who? I didn't see anyone. Got lost, is all." Dean's voice was rough and dry.

"Here." Thomas pulled a water bottle from his coat pocket. Dean grabbed the bottle and began to drink greedily. "Woe, woe, partner. Easy. Slow. Drink it slow." Thomas looked him over. Dean was bruised and battered—a large gash on his head and several cuts. "You, okay? What happened to you, man? You're all beat up."

"I'm not sure what happened. All of a sudden, it was dark, and I was surrounded by trees. I got knocked around, but…why am I bleeding?" Dean asked.

"You've been shot! Looks like a flesh wound, right through the shoulder. You'll be okay. C'mon, let's get you to a medic." Thomas pulled Dean to his feet. "You hear some kinda whistle or something when you were out here?"

"Whistle? You mean, like, for a pretty girl?" Dean asked.

"No. Not like that. I heard something in the woods right before you showed up. It seemed like it might have been far away." Thomas answered. "Big Al went to investigate."

"I didn't hear no whistle. And who's this Al you keep mentioning?" Dean asked.

Thomas helped Dean back to the Buzzard Swamp trailhead. The parking lot was full of activity. An ambulance had arrived along with search and rescue. Although Marion was handcuffed in the back of the sheriff's vehicle, she was the first to see them. "DEAN!"

The first responders ran to Dean, and the EMT's carried him back to their ambulance. Thomas stood at the edge of the dark. The hairs on the back of his neck stood on end. He turned to see Big Al standing beyond the light. Thomas blinked a few times. His mind played tricks as he thought Big Al's eyes were red under the wide-brimmed hat.

"Is that it?" Thomas asked.

"Not quite. There is one more small thing I require." Big Al leaned forward to whisper in Thomas' ear.

Marion struggled to see through the cruiser's back window. She thought she saw Big Al talking with someone she didn't recognize. The door suddenly opened as Big Al slid in beside her.

"Dean. Is he alright?" Marion asked.

"Yes. I think he'll be alright." Big Al smiled. "Don't forget our arraignment."

"What the hell happened?" She asked.

"You're a lucky girl, Marion. Dean planned your murder tonight." Big Al smirked.

"WHAT?! I don't believe you. He would never." She snipped.

"Oh, but he did." Big Al snapped. "He arranged everything. Gasoline doesn't just spill from the pump. But he did accidentally cut his thumb. You think the gun in the glovebox was an accident. He had a handkerchief in the pack, yet he allowed you to open the glove box. It's a clever way to get your prints on it. His blood on the pants in the back seat, gun with your prints, easy frame."

"But the gun is in the glove box. And he's back, unharmed." Marion responded.

"Is it? Is he?" Big Al asked.

Marion watched two deputies leave the back of the ambulance and walk to her Subaru. One opened the passenger's seat and the other to the rear driver's side door.

"What do you think your beloved Dean told them?" Big Al was smiling with a hint of sarcasm.

The two deputies then stepped from her Subaru and stood there scratching their heads. "What?" Marion whispered to herself.

"Don't worry. There's nothing there." Big Al said.

Marion's mind filled with questions. The only one that mattered, she spoke aloud, "When, when am I getting out of here?"

"Well, I'm not sure that you are." Big Al's smile turned with a smirk.

"But our deal? What about our deal?" Her eyes danced around, nervous, twitchy.

Big Al moved right next to her, his face inches from hers. An evil sneer on his face. "The deal was for me to find your boyfriend. I was able to do that. Lucky for you, the poison in those sandwiches didn't kill him."

The whites of her eyes were now visible. "I thought you said..."

Big Al grabbed her by the throat, lifting her off the seat. His mouth nearly touched her cheek as he spoke between gritted teeth. "Don't play games with me, girl. I know what you did, and so does Dean. Luckily, the sandwiches are gone. I gave them to the *LESHY; he* ate them."

Big Al released his grip. Marion slumped back in her seat, tears streaming down her cheeks.

"You're lucky Marion. Dean planned to murder you in the forest. He'd arranged it all. The *LESHY* foiled his plans. Things like that upset the harmony of the woods, and that makes the creature angry." Then Big Al leaned closer to her and sneered, "You will fulfill your oath."

Marion heard a click. Big Al was holding Dean's gun as he cocked the hammer. "Or should I just give this to the police? Your prints are still on the handle. The gloves I'm wearing didn't erase them."

Marion's heart felt like it stopped. Her head dropped as she nodded her agreement.

Big Al's smile returned. "No matter where you are, when I call on you, you will repay your debt." With that, Big Al pushed the car door open and left. Marion looked out every window, but he was gone.

A few seconds later, one of the deputies opened the door and helped her out. "Sorry about this, ma'am. But with your boyfriend's disappearance, we thought it best to detain you." The deputy said as he removed the handcuffs.

"He told us everything. However, we can't find the handgun. Probably lost in the forest." The deputy said.

"Everything?" She asked.

"Yeah. I guess the wild mushrooms he ate were psychedelic. You should be very careful when picking mushrooms in the woods. Some of them can be poisonous. They'll take him to Clarion Hospital if you want to follow." The deputy returned to his patrol car as the ambulance pulled away.

Marion wasn't sure what to do. The backpack and her phone were lost.

Big Al entered the Emporium through the backdoor to find Stormy resting on his recliner. He went to the kitchen and poured himself a cup of coffee. Then he removed the bottle of vodka and a cell phone from the backpack. He unscrewed the bottle's cap which revealed the sound of the seal breaking with the first turn.

Stormy jumped on the counter as Big Al poured the clear liquid into the mug. Then Marion's cell phone began to ring. The caller ID read, Steve. Stormy reached out with a clawed paw to get his attention.

"Yes, yes. I know. Why? I'm not entirely sure. Yes, Dean did seem like a wonderful young man, even if he had murderous intent. Well, perhaps this, Steve," Big Al pointed to the phone's caller ID, "Had some influence on her decision."

Stormy meowed. Big Al scratched her chin, "Yes, I agree, she is treacherous. That's why I liked her so much."

Stormy began to purr. Then she let out a quick meow.

"Well, LESHY's are magical creatures. I really have no idea what a LESHY might like, but I enjoy Kettle One." Big Al said as he took a sip. "Ahhh, so good."

Another meow. Big Al looked at Stormy with a soft smile. "Ah, yes. No, these are just ordinary sunglasses," Big Al said, retrieving the blue lens glasses from his vest pocket, "but they do look vintage, don't they? I'd best put them back."

Big Al was placing the glasses under the counter when he spotted Marion's Subaru pulling from the parking lot. She started down the road when suddenly, she slammed the brakes. There was an old run-down shack where the Emporium had been. Marion whipped into the lot and jumped out of the car. She ran onto the porch to look inside. The windows were busted, and the door was hanging by one hinge.

Her thoughts raced. A gentle breeze came through the trees. She heard a familiar whistle, followed by a quiet voice. "You WILL honor our agreement."

If you want to get a better understanding of why Big AL consulted this book to help Marion, you can get a copy just about anywhere books are sold. You can also find links to purchase by visiting–

alanmcgillbooks.com

IF YOU LOVED THE STYLE AND ATMOSPHERE OF THE HUGH JACKMAN "VAN HELSING"

This book is a must have for fans of A Cry in the Moon's Light. It works like a "the world of" type of concept art book, that you might have seen done with things like *The Witcher* or *Game of Thrones*. It's written from the perspective of a priest who has been documenting strange phenomena. Moreover, the compendium has elements of a "kill book" as a creature weaknesses and strength are described in lovely detail.

**WHAT ARE YOU WAITING FOR?
KEEP GOING**

No Time for Murder

Raymon Tunney finished his shift a troubled man. Ray, as his friends called him, hated working at the prison. You see, Ray put himself through the police academy and was immediately hired in the small borough of Kane. But $7.50 an hour, part-time, doesn't pay the bills. With a young wife and a new house, his dreams started to fade.

Ray couldn't resist the money when SCI Forest was looking for a correctional officer. SCI stands for State Correctional Institution, in case you're wondering. It does have one review and a five-star rating, if you want to look it up.

Anyway, it wasn't the type of law enforcement Ray wanted to do, but the pay was better. The job also came with state benefits and a pension. Despite the financial perks, Ray despised the job. Hard to be locked in with criminals day in and day out, not to mention the inmates.

The afternoon shift was nearly over, but Ray left early. He drove across the road to the Kwik-fil to fill up his truck. Yes, the same Route 66 Kwik-fil where these stories begin to take a turn.

The big Ford was a gas hog, and he needed to fill it, two sometimes three times a week. He flipped the handle, but the pump didn't turn on. His watch read 10:30. *What gives?* Ray thought.

He ran into the store, but there was no sign of the clerk. The store was open, or the doors would have been locked. He waited a few moments, then got a six-pack from the cooler. He returned to the front, but the clerk still wasn't there. *Odd*, he thought. Roberta checked him out every night. *Where was she?*

Ray set the six-pack on the counter and went to the back. *Maybe she's in the bathroom.* Ray knocked at the women's room, "BERT? YOU IN THERE?" but there was no answer. "

He noticed the office door was open. Ray looked inside, but she wasn't in there either. The monitors glitched, which drew his attention. He could see his truck at the pump, inside the store, and at the back of the building, but no Roberta.

He didn't feel like waiting, so he left. Marienville was in the opposite direction, but he wanted to fill his truck before going home. While he was there, he could grab a drink. He could use one after the day he just had.

Route 66 was clear under the star-filled sky. Ray pulled from the Kwik Fill lot slowly and easily. The State Police liked to sit in dark spots along the way, and he didn't feel like dealing with them. His head was on a swivel, especially after what happened at work today.

He passed the VFW a few minutes later. There weren't any cars in the lot. Another oddity. That club was always busy on a Friday night.

Less than a minute later, he entered Marienville and pulled to the gas pump of the town's only convenience store. Ray got out and placed the nozzle into his fuel tank. He flipped the pump to turn it on, but nothing happened. A small sign read, please pre-pay after dark. *Even with a card?* Ray thought.

Ray went inside, "HELLO?", but it was empty, just like the Kwik Fill.

Ray got back in his truck and turned the key. The old F150 didn't want to start. Another twist of the key, but the engine hesitated. "What the…?" Then, the heavy vehicle's engine started. Ray pulled out and drove down the street to the Kelly Hotel. Ray was a little nervous about shutting the truck off, but the neon beer lights were on, and he knew this place didn't close until midnight.

Ray went inside to find this place was empty too. "ANYBODY HERE?" No reply. Ray was perplexed now. He went back to his truck and tried the key. The response was clicking. The battery still functioned, but the engine wouldn't turn over.

Then he heard the low hum of music down the street. Ray could see it was coming from Lucky's Pub. The neon sign was lit, and the front door was open. *Everybody must be in there.*

Ray hustled across the street and reached for the screen door when he noticed the shop beside Lucky's. A giant neon sign read Emporium, with a smaller sign in the front window reading OPEN. *I never saw that before,* he thought.

The screen door slammed and bounced behind after he went through. Like every other place he'd been in this night, the place was empty. Not one person was seated at the bar. Half-full glasses of beer and whisky, burning cigarettes sat in ashtrays, but the bar was empty. *What is going on around here?* He mused.

Ray sat on a stool to wait. A voice behind startled him. "Quiet night, eh friend?" An older man took a seat around the corner from Ray. A small chin was visible behind a snow-white goatee that matched his hair. His eyes seemed to glow under the shadow created by his wide-brimmed hat.

The song on the jukebox ended as the man walked past Ray. The man went behind the bar to pour himself a cup of coffee. He then opened a blue bottle and poured a white liquid into the coffee. He turned to Ray and asked, "What can I get you, friend?"

"Do, do you work here? Where's Bill?" Ray asked. "And where is everybody? The town is dead. Why isn't there anybody at the convenience store?"

"I help out on slow nights," the man started. I own the shop next door. Well, more accurately, I run the shop next door." He extended his hand across the bar. "Most call me Big Al."

Ray reluctantly shook the stranger's hand. "I've never seen you around here before."

Big Al smiled. "I'm sure you have friend; you probably just hadn't noticed. They say a troubled mind tends to be more focused."

"I'm not troubled! There's nothing wrong with me." Ray objected. "Why haven't you answered my question? There was nobody at the Kwik Fill. I had to come the whole way into town for gas, and nobody was there either. The Kelly is dead. I come in here, and it's empty."

"I wouldn't exactly call it empty. I'm here." Big Al smiled. "I don't know about anyone else; I've been here with you." Big Al answered.

"Yeah, well, it's a little weird. Everything's open, but nobody's around. My reliable truck suddenly won't start, and why do you keep calling me friend? I don't know you." Ray snipped.

"Are you sure about that?" Big Al's grin faded.

Ray scoffed, "Yeah, I'm sure."

"Perhaps you should have a drink to calm your nerves." Big Al stated.

Ray looked around skeptically before asking, "What are you drinking?"

Big Al raised his cup, "Coffee. And a bit of Five Farms. I know it's late for the caffeine, but I suspect it will be a long night for you and me."

"I'll have a Straub," Ray responded. "And it ain't gonna be long for me; I'm having this one, then heading home."

"If you say so, friend. One Straub coming up." Big Al went to the coolers at the bar's base, pulled out a bottle of the lager, and set it in front of Ray beside a glass.

Ray didn't bother with the glass; he took a swig from the bottle. He started to reach into his pocket when Big Al put up a hand to stop him. "This one's on me, friend,"

"No, no. I work at the prison. I can't be taking free drinks. I shouldn't be in here in the first place." Ray responded sharply, flopping several bills on the bar.

"I said no money." Big Al's response was immediate, and his voice boomed. Then, his expression lightened as his lips curled into a smile. "You won't owe me anything. It's just a polite tavern custom. You can buy the next round. Besides, your boss will never know. And he's done far worse than accept a free drink at a local bar." Big Al's eyes glowed under the shadow of his hat. His expression was stoic. Big Al took a sip from his mug before speaking again. "Now, what troubles you? You didn't come here, still in uniform, risking discipline, if you hadn't a long day. Perhaps I can help?"

"What? What do you mean far worse? How? What do you know about it?" Ray's mind was flustered, and his nerves were starting to fray.

"Oh, I dunno. Try me. What have you to lose?" Big Al smirked as he took another sip of his spiked coffee.

Ray glanced at the clock hanging above the bar, 11:18, took a big sigh, and then explained everything. It's hard to say why he decided to unburden himself; after all, Big Al was a stranger. But for the next 45 minutes, Ray told him everything.

Big Al took a sip of his spiked coffee. "Well, that's quite a story, friend. What are you going to do?"

Ray was now on his third beer. He took a big swallow and shook his head. "What can I do? If I say anything, they'll fire me. If I say nothing...it could be something much worse."

The sound of two car doors interrupted Ray's thought. He jumped off the barstool to peek out the front door. He could see his truck at the Kelly Hotel, and now a car was parked next to it.

Ray stepped back. "Oh shit."

"What's the matter?" Big Al asked.

"That looks like the car from one of the guys at work. I told my boss I needed to get home early to watch my kids. If he catches me in here having a drink and in uniform to boot…"

"Go in there and lock the stall door." Big Al pointed to the sign hanging above the restrooms, *Shidders*. "I'll come get you when it's safe."

Ray scurried into the men's room and sat on the commode. The screen door banged twice as he slid the bolt to lock the stall. The jukebox started again, and Ray heard the loud break of a cue ball striking balls on the table.

Seconds seemed like minutes as he sat and waited. The bathroom door opened, temporarily making the music louder. Ray leaned down to look under the stall. Two legs with the shoes facing him were there. Ray sat back up quickly, his heart beating faster.

"Looks like it might be a while. Meet me at the shop next door. If you go right now, you won't be noticed." It was Big Al.

The music got loud when the door opened, then quieted again after it shut. Ray let a short time elapse before he opened the stall door. He could hear pool sticks and Van Halen's "Runnin' with the Devil" on the jukebox.

Ray stepped into the small vestibule and peered toward the back. He couldn't see anyone; this was his chance. He quickly went to the screen door and went out. Ray carefully held the door as it closed so there was no loud bang.

The Emporium light was still on, so Ray opened that door, and went in. The chime of the overhead bell startled him. "AHH." His heart missed a beat at the sight of the giant Poliger towering over him. "What the hell is that?"

Ray composed himself and then slid the door lock. He searched the window area for a switch to turn off the neon signs when Big Al spoke, "There's no need for that friend. Nobody is going to find you in here."

Big Al stood behind a counter in the back of the store. Ray's mind couldn't understand what he saw. Big Al was three times as far as he'd expected. He believed the store to be the same dimensions as Lucky's, yet the distance to Big Al was much farther away.

Big Al waved for him to come to the counter. Ray abandoned his desire to turn off the neon signs and weaved through the various displays. His eyes caught glimpses of incredible things. Odd taxidermy, like the giant Poliger. Strange weapons of the like he'd never seen. And curious symbols etched on patches, clothing, and other items.

"You're safe in here, Ray." Big Al took a long drink from his mug.

Ray reached the counter in seconds. He looked back, trying to make sense of the distance and how he could have crossed the span so quickly. "Friend?" Big Al interrupted his thoughts.

Ray hesitated as he spoke. "You, you said you could help me. Hey, ah, before we get into that, what is that damned thing?" Ray pointed to the giant beast at the front of the store.

"The Poliger?" Big Al's smile broadened.

"A Pol…a…ger?" Ray tried to understand, but he could barely pronounce the word.

"A big game hunter came across it in Siberia. Magnificent, isn't she." Big Al beamed.

"Ah, okay. You sayin' that's a real…animal? Or was a real animal?" Ray questioned.

"Is that really why you are here? To discuss taxidermy?" Big Al took another sip.

Ray kept looking at the giant creature until he finally snapped out of it. "Ah, no. No. At the bar, you said you could help me?"

Big Al's eyes began to change ever so slightly. "The issue at work?"

"Yeah, like I told you at the bar, the counselor and my supervisor," Ray stated.

"Inmates?" Big Al asked.

"What? No, the hell with them. They're a bunch of animals." Ray responded. "I can't let them get away with it."

"Sounds like the counselor needs to go, and you need a new boss." Big Al grinned.

"Now you're getting to it." Ray felt like Big Al finally understood.

"You want to eliminate this counselor? Your boss?" Big Al looked Ray up and down, "or both?"

"Isn't that what we're discussing?" Ray snapped.

Big Al wasn't having any of it. "I'm no assassin. You misunderstood my offer and the nature of this place. Besides, you don't need me for something like that. Use the, what was your term? The animals? Get them to take care of it."

"No inmate can be trusted. They'd take care of them alright, but they'd turn on me just for fun." Ray spouted.

"Why is this your problem? What do you care?" Big Al said.

"Because I can't bear the thought of some of them getting out. Help me before anyone else gets hurt." Ray's tone softened, and Big Al took it all in.

"I can offer suggestions and supply you with the means, but you must carry it out." Big Al sneered. His friendly disposition was gone.

Ray's eyes spotted two glass bottles on a shelf behind Big Al, "What are those?"

One bottle was sealed with a purple cork. It contained a neon green liquid. Beside it was a small glass vial with a glowing red liquid. "Is that leaking?" Ray pointed to the vial as smoke came from under the cork.

"No, it's fine. Moisture accumulates around the cap. The heat of the vial causes it to evaporate, creating the mist you see." Big Al responded.

Beside the glass bottles, there was additional shelving filled with numerous pots containing plants and vines. A few growing lamps allowed Ray to view the flourishing vegetation. The entire section appeared to be an unruly mess to the untrained eye.

"What's that?" Ray pointed to the one that stood out. A singular plant bore purple flowers in the center of this makeshift greenhouse. The dark petals accentuated its yellow style and filaments.

"Ahh, the Nightshade." Big Al answered. "The plant is toxic. They say ten of its berries is enough to kill a man."

"Berries?" Ray asked.

"Yes. They resemble blueberries." Big Al responded.

"Do you have any?" Ray noticed a jar sitting next to the plant as he asked the question. The grow light above revealed it was filled with dark berries. "Are those?"

"Well, lookie there. I didn't realize there were any in the shop." Big Al acted surprised, but Ray knew better.

"How much for the whole jar?" Ray asked.

"They're not for sale. Nothing in here is for sale." Big Al said.

"Isn't this a store?" Ray asked. "C'mon, seriously. How much?" Ray pulled a wade of cash from his pocket and thumbed through the bills.

"Tell you what, friend. I'll give you the entire jar on one condition." The corners of Big Al's mouth began to form a smile. "You can have the jar in exchange for a favor."

"A favor?" Ray didn't like the idea of owing anyone. He knew firsthand what those kinds of arrangements were like at the prison. But Ray's mind turned, knowing this might solve all his problems. "What kind of favor?"

"Hard to say. I assure you, it won't be anything you can't handle." Big Al sneered and then tilted his head. His eyes glowed in a sinister way as he vocalized the next part. "You want to kill that woman? Get her to eat ten of these," Big Al picked up the jar and pointed to the berries inside, "and all your troubles will be gone. But she must eat ten. No more, no less."

"Alright," Ray said.

"Alright, what?" Big Al asked.

Ray extended his hand, "We have a deal. Give me the berries."

Big Al took Ray's hand and yanked him close. The smile was gone, and there was no smirk. Everything was deadly serious. "You take this jar; you agree to the terms of our arrangement. No matter what I ask of you, no matter when I ask, you WILL do it."

The intensity in Big Al's eyes did not waver as he released Ray's hand. Ray, on the other hand, trembled. He knew the deal he'd made would exact a heavy toll.

"Tell me, Ray," It was the first time Big Al called him by his first name, "Why are you concerned about the other guards? They don't like monsters any more than you. Don't you think they'd be on your side?"

"I told you my boss Mike, he's asshole buddies with the warden. If that piece of shit doesn't like you, he'll put you in with the murders and sodomites, if not worse." Ray responded.

"Forest is a maximum-security prison. What could be worse than that?" Big Al asked.

"A transfer to the supermax. Greene. The nastiest of the nasties." Ray said.

"Wouldn't that take the Secretary of Corrections?" Big Al took another sip of his coffee. "Doesn't she hate the warden?"

"That's what the rumors are. She likes to embarrass him at state-wide meetings, but nothing ever happens. The warden's one of these guys who should never have gotten promoted. Now he's listening to this dipshit counselor who thinks pedophiles should be reclassified as Minor Attracted Persons. They're recommending early releases." Ray stared at the jar of berries, "I can't let that happen."

Big Al raised his mug, "Just don't forget our deal," then smiled, "Good luck."

Ray nodded and went to the door. The bell rang as he opened and closed it. Big Al walked to the front and watched from the window. Stormy, his cat, was on the counter and reached out with her claws to get his attention.

He set the mug down and picked her up, cradling her in his arms. She began to purr as they watched Ray walk across the street and enter his truck. Stormy meowed as Ray turned north on Route 66 and drove out of sight.

The next day, Ray arrived at work early. He needed to be there before the counselor and his boss left. Ray brought his lunch in a brown paper bag and carried another with seven plastic sandwich baggies full of blueberries. Two of the baggies contained ten Nightshade berries mixed in with blueberries. He'd marked them with a red line.

Big Al picked up his coffee from the counter and carried Stormy back to his domicile behind the counter. Confused? Don't be. Time works differently in the Emporium. They both watched Ray disappear into the night as written two paragraphs ago, but by the time Big Al was at the back of the store, the next day already occurred, and Ray's Nightshade mission was complete.

Big Al poured fresh coffee into the mug, then added two shots of Five Farms Cream Liqueur. "Ahh, finest there is, eh Stormy?"

He set the cat down and picked up the Derrick Newspaper dated Tuesday, July 23rd. The front-page headline read, MURDER AT SCI FOREST. "Well, Stormy. This is somewhat unexpected. It seems Ray didn't listen to what I told him. Listen to this: SCI Forest Psychologist and licensed sex therapist Linda Albright was found dead in her office Tuesday afternoon. Sources close to the investigation tell us she was stabbed to death by an inmate who feared an early release. Inmate Thomas H. Green told investigators he enjoyed watching women having sex with animals, something he claims was the result of abuse by former employers. Green told investigators Albright was lobbying to have the term bestiality changed to AAP animal-attracted persons.

Despite his disease, Green knew it was a sin and morally wrong. He further stated that nobody with his condition should ever be released into society and that Albright's attempt to justify these horrid acts was equally bad. Green stabbed Albright 107 times with a letter opener before violating her corpse.

But that wasn't the only thing that occurred Tuesday; corrections officer Ray Tunney and his boss, Sargent Michael Binder, were found unconscious in the breakroom. Authorities are unclear as to the cause at this time. Details of this investigation are ongoing. Well, Stormy, those certainly are interesting events." Big Al folded the paper and then picked up the telephone.

The old rotary phone dialed slowly but true. A few rings later, "SCI Forest, how may I direct your call?"

"Hello, Phyllis." Big Al responded.

The phone was silent, but Big Al could hear Phyllis's heavy breathing on the other end of the line. Several agonizing moments passed before her dry lips parted. " He...hello. It's you, isn't it?"

"Why, Phyllis, so very nice to hear your voice again. How is the chair? Does it still provide the relief you sought?" Big Al's voice was sincere but also sinister. "It's time, dear Phyllis."

Phyliss' eyes closed hard. Her mouth completely dry as she took a big gulp of air. "What do you need?"

Big Al explained everything to Phyllis in great detail. She did not argue or barter. After he was done, Big Al placed the receiver on the cradle without so much as a goodbye. The phone then rang most violently. The receiver bounced on the cradle with each ring. One, two, three, four, five, then Big Al answered. "Hello, Ray."

"Hey fuck you. The deal's off. An inmate with a conscience killed Albright. And the berries didn't kill my boss, so…"

"Our arrangement was for the jar. How you used them was your business. The deal was never contingent upon your success. It was merely for their purchase." Big Al sneered.

"Yeah, well, I'm not doing anything for you. I damn near lost my life because of those damn things. I'd say we're even." Ray sniped.

"As you wish, Ray." Big Al hung up the phone as Stormy touched his arm. Big Al picked her up with his coffee mug and took another sip. He carried her to his recliner in the back room. Big Al snapped his fingers, and the television turned on. It was the local evening news for August 22nd on WTAJ. The anchorman opened the broadcast with, *"Tonight's top story, Correctional Officer Ray Tunney was arrested today in connection with the attempted poisoning of his boss, Michael Binder. According to the probable cause affidavit, Tunney gave Binder a snack bag of blueberries, which also contained the poisonous Nightshade berries. According to the charging documents, Tunney also consumed a few berries to cover up the crime, hoping investigators would see him as a victim, too. He initially claimed no knowledge of the toxic berries in the bag, but after a prison secretary confessed to selling him the berries, Tunney confessed."*

Big Al snapped his finger again to turn off the television. His eyes glowed as he raised the mug to his lips. Stormy meowed. "What's that? Ah well, I'm pretty sure he was never going to honor our agreement anyway. Don't worry. Phyliss will be alright if she does exactly what I instructed. Ray, on the other hand, will have a hard time being one of them now. I doubt he'll survive the night."

Werewolves & Witches

BOOK ONE IN THE HORROR ROMANCE SAGA
People love it, and so will you.

★★★★★

ABSOLUTELY AMAZING!

Honestly no positive review could do this story justice. Can't wait for more!

★★★★★

A brilliant, shocking, and immensely engaging read...A MUST READ!
The horror, the scares, the heart, all of it wouldn't have been possible without such strong characters and their bond to one another. A Cry in the Moon's Light is a must-read paranormal fantasy and romance reader.

As Bob Seger once said,
Turn the Page!

EYE FOR TROUBLE

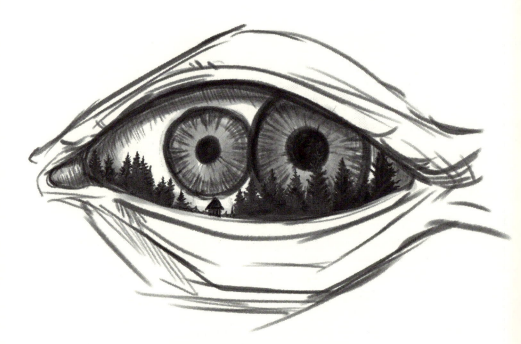

Hot summer days can be dangerous. The pavement gets so hot it's hard to walk in bare feet. The sun can burn your skin to a crisp red, not to mention how it heats up a bicycle seat.

Kids love it just the same, though. Summer marks the end of the school year in late May or early June, depending on where you are. The freedom it brings is rarely felt by anyone but a kid. No homework, no bullies, and no bells!

Tommy and Phyliss were best friends. During the school year, Tommy spent hours in the computer lab hanging out with the nerdy kids. The school only had 5 computers, usually occupied by juniors and seniors, so he took whatever time he could get.

Phyliss, on the other hand, wasn't interested in electronics. Her thoughts lay elsewhere, like boys. She was a year older than Tommy and a middle school cheerleader. She was a pretty girl with long blonde hair who'd developed a crush on Jimmy Wayne, the sophomore quarterback.

But when summer began, Phyliss and Tommy were inseparable—it had been like that since they were little. Tommy's family bought a finished basement a couple of miles away from Phyliss's farm, and Tommy's dad was in the process of building the house over the foundation.

Tommy met Phyliss after his mom developed a friendship with Phyliss' mom. She sold Tupperware door to door for extra money as the farm wasn't that profitable. Eager to find him friends in this rural area, Tommy's mom would drive him to the farm so they could play together. As they got older, Tommy would ride his bike to Phyliss's house.

This year's school year ended like all the others, a few days into June and blisteringly hot. The phone rang, and Phyliss knew exactly who it was. "Hello."

"You want to go swimming today?" Tommy asked excitedly.

"Sure." Phyliss was excited, too, but for a much different reason. She'd hoped Jimmy would be there. Tommy, however, did not.

Phyliss didn't or couldn't see it. Tommy was bullied like the rest of his computer lab buddies, and Jimmy Wayne was the leader of the crew that bullied them. Summer was always a welcome relief because none of the bullies were around. But in town, there was always a chance he'd run into them, especially at the pool.

It was hot and Tommy was willing to take the chance. "Great, I'll leave now."

Phyliss waited impatiently for Tommy to arrive. She was outside on the back porch when he rode up the drive. "What took you so long?" She didn't wait for a reply. Her leg was over the frame, and she pedaled away before he was stopped. They raced down her drive and onto the blacktop at blinding speed—well, blinding for middle schoolers.

They took turns leading the way. One would get tired, and the other would jump in front. They kept leapfrogging on Greely Farm Road until it turned onto Walnut. Tommy kept the lead all the way to Park Circle.

The community pool was on the other side of town. All he needed to do was make it inside the pool before Wayne and his crew showed up. Once inside the grounds, he'd be safe. The lifeguards wouldn't tolerate any trouble.

It took them about an hour to reach town, and Tommy stopped his bike at Park Circle. Marienville wasn't a big place, and Park Circle was an open area providing a good view of the main intersection.

"What's wrong? Why'd you stop?" Phyllis asked as she pulled up beside him.

"Nothin', just waiting for you." Tommy was embarrassed about the harassment. Phyliss was his closest friend, and he didn't want her to know he was afraid.

She laughed before pushing off the pedal, lurching the bike ahead. "C'mon on then. Maybe you need to catch up!"

Tommy jumped on the pedal, bolting forward to catch her. She never touched the brakes, rocketing across Route 66. He feathered the brakes, slowing to look both ways. Seeing it was clear, he crossed the road, racing even harder to reach her. He watched Phyliss round the corner ahead. By the time he entered the intersection, she had passed the Marienville library and turned into the MACA Community Pool's parking lot.

Both were hungry from the long ride. Tommy's mother had given him twenty dollars to buy lunch. The two sat under the pavilion with a slice of pizza and orange soda. Life was good until he heard the low rumble of a 79 Gremlin, and then his pulse increased.

"Tommy. Tommy, are you listening?" Phyliss pulled on his arm. "Ugh. I'm going to the bathroom."

Tommy hadn't heard a word Phyliss said. He knew the sound of Jimmy's car, and his eyes fixed on the Gremlin as it drove through the parking lot. It stopped on the other side of the office building, and he recognized the sound of car doors shutting.

Jimmy and three of his companions got out, flopping beach towels over their shoulders. They were as cocky a bunch as you'd ever come across. Even more so today.

Tommy's stomach churned as he took stock of everyone here. The grounds weren't busy, as only a few families were at the pool today. It was mostly mothers with young children and no dads since it was a workday. He'd need to rely on the lifeguards to keep him safe.

Tommy took his beach towel to a patch of ground behind the lifeguard chair. Jimmy wouldn't do anything if he was near her. Hopefully, Phyllis will come out of the bathroom soon and join him.

Jimmy and his three friends came through the turnstile and immediately spotted him. It was as if they knew he was here. Jimmy's face was covered in a big grin as he pointed at Tommy. His three friends erupted in laughter at the comment.

Then, their attention was diverted as Phyliss came out of the girl's bathroom Jimmy and his boys. The moment she saw Jimmy, her demeanor changed. She began to twirl her hair shyly and shuffle as she greeted him. "Hi, Jimmy."

Tommy couldn't hear what they were saying, but he could tell she was flirting, and he didn't like it. A feeling of resentment and jealousy rose in him. *How could she like somebody like him? Guys an asshole.* He thought.

"Hey there, Phyliss." Jimmy took her hands and leaned back to look her up and down. "I like your suit. It's very sexy."

Tommy watched as his blood boiled. She was giggling and twirling her hair like a child. Laughing at his ridiculous jokes and touching his arm with each smile. A few minutes later, Jimmy put his arm around Phyliss and began to steer her toward the lifeguard changing room.

Jimmy's companions giggled and elbowed each other. That's when Tommy noticed Jimmy's red swim trunks. His heart sank. These were the same type of trunks worn by the lifeguards.

Tommy took a few steps across the pavement toward the pavilion. After Jimmy and Phyliss entered the changing room, he saw the door shut. Jimmy's three friends had their ears pressed against it.

"Where's Phyliss?" Tommy asked. His voice crackled.

"What's it to you geek?" One of Jimmy's friends took a step toward him.

Fear welled up inside. A nauseated feeling ran through his stomach, and then the door burst open. Phyliss ran from the pitch-black room and straight to the exit. Her hand was over her mouth, and she was sobbing. The strap of her bathing suit was torn, and she nearly caught one in the tines on the turnstile as she rushed through.

Jimmy emerged from the door frame, calling to her, "Phyliss, c'mon. It's all good, babe."

The next few seconds were a blur for Tommy. He didn't realize what happened until after. People would later tell the story of a young boy with black hair who grabbed an empty soda bottle off the picnic table and smashed the face of the star quarterback.

The impact was swift and hard, and there was a loud clunk as the bottle broke Jimmy's nose. Bone shattered, blood spurted, and Jimmy Wayne gasped before grabbing his face. Jimmy's eyes watered, and the searing pain caused him to collapse into the darkened room.

Nobody saw that coming. Nobody expected to see the town bully get dumped on his ass by a scrawny farm boy. They hadn't seen what Jimmy did to Phyliss, which made Tommy's assault a complete shock.

Tommy didn't hesitate. He dropped the bottle and ran through the turnstile before anyone could move. "GET HIMMMMM!" Jimmy screamed. He'd staggered to the door frame, holding his nose. Before any of his crew could react, Tommy tied the turnstile with his beach towel. None of the tines would rotate, and they couldn't get out.

Tommy rushed to Phyliss, who was still sobbing on her bike. "Are you okay? What happened?" Tommy took off his shirt and gave it to her.

She pulled the shirt over her head, fighting back more tears. "I'm okay. Let's get outta here."

Jimmy's crew was yanking on the turnstile, but they couldn't get it to budge. By then, Jimmy was standing at the fence. His face looked awful. Exposed bone, cartilage, and pink tissue, along with plenty of blood, the once handsome young man, grotesque. "I'm gonna kill you. You hear me. You little creep! YOU HEAR ME! YOU'RE DEAD!"

Tommy hadn't really seen the damage until now, and it was gruesome. He turned to Phyliss, "We gotta go!" Phyliss didn't need any encouragement, and she started pedaling right away. Tommy jumped on his bike and followed.

The two pedaled as fast as they could out of the parking lot. They rushed past the library, then turned toward Route 66. Neither bothered to look both ways as they fled across. Once they reached the park, Tommy slammed on the brakes, and vomited.

Phyliss stopped when she realized Tommy was still behind. She turned around and peddled back to him, "C'mon. We gotta get the hell outta here before they come."

Tommy knew they couldn't go straight home. Jimmy would catch them for sure. Their only chance was to find a place to hide, wait until the Gremlin passed, and take the long way home.

Tommy didn't have anything to wipe his mouth, and he was forced to spit chunks until the vomit was gone. He nodded to Phyliss as they both began to pedal away. Tommy moved in front of her, "Not that way. Follow me."

Tommy led them down West Spruce Street, and that's when he first saw it. He slowed the bike for a better look at the rundown shack with the big neon sign. It sat on the corner of West Spruce and Hemlock. The sign read Emporium of Curiosities, Oddities, and Strange Things.

Tommy brought his bike to a stop half a block away. Phyliss stopped next to him. "What's that place? I didn't notice it before."

Tommy just shook his head. Phyliss looked back nervously, "Where is he? I don't hear the car?"

The two friends looked over the entire area, but nobody was around. Jimmy's car should have been at the intersection by now, but it wasn't. And there was no traffic anywhere.

As their eyes surveyed the big intersection, a small dust devil appeared. It traveled down the middle of Route 66 until it was out of sight. Right after the first disappeared, a second larger swirling cloud followed as if chasing the smaller one.

A hot breeze came through the park and hit the two friends in the face. Then, the park became eerily quiet. There was no breeze, no sound, just the hot sun beating down.

Unexpectedly, a voice came from nowhere. "Everything alright?" They turned to see a man seated on a rocking chair on the porch of the small shack.

The man struck a long match on the wall and used it to light the bowl of a curved pipe. With each inhale, the glow would become more pronounced. The amber coals reflected in his eyes. Then Tommy smelled the aroma of cherry as the smoke billowed.

The man's long-brim hat shadowed his face even on this bright day. On his lap was a sliver cat he was petting. Seconds later, the man rose and went to the door, still holding the cat. He turned the knob, then looked at them before saying, "Come inside. You both look thirsty. I'll give you something cool to drink."

After the man was inside, Tommy got off his bike and started toward the shack. Phyliss grabbed his arm, "I don't think we should go in there."

She barely finished the last syllable when the wind picked up again. This time, they heard Jimmy's Gremlin. It was faint but definitely the same throaty muffler and it seemed to be coming from East Spruce Street.

Tommy looked back at Phyliss. He didn't understand the thoughts or feelings, but he wasn't afraid. He looked toward the car's sound, knowing Phyliss could hear it too. "I think we're better off in there."

Tommy walked his bike to the back of the little shop. He laid it on the grass and waved for Phyliss to do the same. "C'mon. Put your bike back here so Jimmy doesn't see it."

Phyliss looked toward the intersection of Route 66 one more time, swallowed, and then reluctantly did as Tommy suggested. The two friends walked to the porch nervously, looking around. "I've never seen this place, have you?"

Tommy shrugged, "No, but it's a store. If those guys can't find us, it's good enough for me. Let's get something to drink. We can hide out in there until Jimmy leaves. It shouldn't be too long."

Tommy turned the doorknob and pushed. The door struck a bell hanging above and gave a loud chime. The sound lingered as they walked in. Tommy pushed the door shut, and the bell chimed again.

"AHHHHH!" They both shrieked at the sight of the Poliger towering over them. Tommy clutched his heart when he realized the creature wasn't alive. "What the hell is that!?" Phyliss asked.

Tommy stepped slowly toward the giant taxidermy, "Tommy, don't." Phyliss begged.

He shrugged her off to gingerly touch the giant beast. His hand melted into thick white fur. "It's some kinda bear, I think." He remarked. "Very muscular."

A voice in the back of the store provided a better answer, "It's a Poliger. Don't worry, it won't hurt you."

Tommy and Phyliss were startled by the voice. Tommy immediately withdrew his hand and moved away. Both looked in the direction of the voice to see the same man from the porch behind a counter at the rear of the store. Tommy did a double take. *This store isn't that big.* Unable to reconcile the distance, Tommy decided to look outside. The door chimed again. Tommy walked around the side to get a better look at the length of the building. It wasn't more than twenty feet. Yet when he returned to the inside, the man standing behind the counter appeared three times as far as that.

Tommy glanced at the Poliger, which was now on all fours. The snarling creature no longer looked menacing but appeared pleasant, almost smiling. "What the…how'd that get…?" Tommy's question trailed off.

"Huh?" Phyliss noticed it, too. "That thing was standing on its hind legs. Its claws were coming at us, and the fangs were showing… right?"

"Come now, children, be not afraid. Grab a stool and let me get you something to drink on this hot day."

Neither Tommy nor Phyliss understood any of this. Tommy knew the building was not that big; he'd gone outside to double-check. The place wasn't much bigger than Phyliss's chicken coop, yet inside, it was the size of a barn.

Phyliss grabbed Tommy's arm as she followed behind. The two slowly walked through the rows of shelves, each containing various weird items neither of them had ever seen.

Phyliss squeezed his arm, "Is that the same guy from outside? He's wearing a pink and white shirt now."

"Yeah, he looks like an old bartender, with those armbands and the yellow straw hat," Tommy remarked.

"Soda fountain." Big Al said. "This is the uniform of a Soda Jerk."

Tommy and Phyliss looked at each other. She whispered directly into Tommy's ear and barely heard his reply. *How did this guy hear what we said?*

"Grab a shirt off the clearance rack son." Big Al pointed to some shirts on hangers beside them, then he pointed to a sign on the wall. No shoes, no shirt, no barter.

"Wait, this is your shirt. I'll grab one." Phyliss whispered. Tommy stopped her, "No. Not in here. I'll just put on one of these."

"But you don't have any money. You spend it all on our lunch." Phyliss remarked.

Big Al continued wiping the counter with a wet cloth as he spoke, "You have nothing to worry about with me. But I'm afraid Thomas is right. Keep your shirt on, and he can put on one of those. Don't worry about payment. I'm sure we'll work something out."

Tommy reached for a plain white shirt from the rack and slid it over his shoulders. "Do you know me, mister?"

"I know everyone that comes into my store." Big Al smiled.

Tommy moved closer to the counter on the right. Under the glass, he could see rectangular objects neatly placed on the shelf.

"Are these movie props mister?" Tommy asked.

Big Al let out a chuckle. "No, I'm afraid not. They are communication devices. They're not yet…available to you."

"Communication devices? You mean, like communicators?" Tommy's eyes beamed with excitement.

"Like your favorite show? Star Trek." Big Al smirked.

When Tommy and Phyliss looked up, Big Al was standing behind the counter in front of them. *How'd he get over here so fast?* Tommy thought.

"How do you know that's my favorite show?" Tommy was starting to get a little nervous.

A friendly smile showed behind his silver beard as his eyes twinkled. "Allow me to introduce myself. I am Big Al, the Dream Maker. And this is my Emporium. The Emporium of Curiosities, Oddities, and Strange Things." Big Al said with the tip of his hat. "Now, how about some ice cream?"

Phyliss and Tommy looked at the location where they first saw Big Al when they entered. Both blinked and rubbed their eyes. Big Al was once again standing at the end of the counter, with soda machines behind and a red countertop in front.

The two friends looked at each other skeptically, but young minds are often distracted. Their apprehension was diminished by a warm smile and the mention of ice cream.

Tommy and Phyliss sat right in front of Big Al. The mood lightened as the anger and fear seemingly gone. Their eyes wandered, taking in all the sights and sounds of this vintage soda shop.

Big Al reached under the bar and pulled out a Vanilla Fizz for Tommy. "How'd you know? That's my favorite. When I visit my grandmother, she sends me to the drugstore for cigarettes. She gives me enough money to buy a Vanilla Fizz. They call me the Vanilla Fizz Kid there." Tommy paused, a bit disappointed, "Like I said, I don't have any money, mister."

"Don't worry about that now." Big Al smiled. "Maybe someday you can return the favor." But the smile looked a little different this time. "Call me Big Al."

Then Big Al reached under the counter and retrieved a hot fudge sundae for Phyliss. This, too, was her favorite, but she wasn't as easily swayed as Tommy. Her eyes showed distrust. Big Al could only grin. He grabbed a spoon from behind the counter and dipped into her sundae. He took the bite and threw the spoon in a sink behind the bar.

"There's nothing wrong with your sundae, I promise you. It's just ice cream and hot fudge. Go ahead, dig in. You've had a rough day." Big Al's eyes were warm, and his tone soft. You both have." This put her at ease so she could enjoy the treat in front of her.

As the two enjoyed their desserts, Big Al slipped to the back room. Phyliss leaned to Tommy and whispered, "Did you see his eyes?"

"You mean the way they changed color?" Tommy responded.

"No. He's got two iris' and two pupils in his left eye." Phyliss peered around Tommy to make sure Big Al wasn't coming. "It's like the smaller one was ducking behind the bigger one." She was about to go on but stopped when Big Al flipped back the curtains and returned.

Afraid Big Al may have heard, Tommy said the first thing that came to his mind. "This is the best Vanilla Fizz I've ever had. I think it's better than the drug store at my grandma's."

"I'm glad you like it," Big Al said, then looked at Phyliss. "What Jimmy Wayne did was wrong, but you survived. You'll be stronger for it."

Phyliss set the spoon on the counter. Her eyes hardened as she addressed Big Al's comment. "I know. I was scared, and he ripped my suit, but nothing happened. I crushed his balls with my knee, then ran out. It's just that…I thought he was a great guy. Turns out he's just a creep. But I can't go back to school if he's there. It's humiliating."

"What are you talking about? You have to go to school. Look, I'm not going to let anything happen to you. You're my best friend. I'll protect you." Tommy meant every word, but Phyliss knew better.

"I know you would, but you'll just get hurt. He's too big," Phyliss said.

"I did pretty good today, didn't I?" Tommy snapped.

Phyliss put a soft hand on his arm, then stood to ask Big Al. "Do you have a bathroom I can use?"

Big Al pointed to the back. "Stormy will show you the way."

"Stormy?" Phyliss was confused until she felt a pinch on her leg. The gray Manx reached out with her claws to get Phyliss's attention.

Phyliss bent down and stroked the cat's fur. "Well, hello. Aren't you precious. Are you going to show me the way?"

Stormy walked in front, and Phyliss followed. The little cat led her to a dark hallway with the sign *Shidders.*

Tommy never took his eyes off her until she disappeared into the shadows. He slurped the last of his drink and then set the glass down. Big Al placed it in the sink and then wiped the area before Tommy.

He motioned with the rag toward the front door. "I'd say Lilly likes you."

Tommy turned his head. His eyes scanned the entire front and then gleaned the rest of the store. "Where's the…what did you call it? Pol something?"

"Lilly. She's a Poliger, or was, the last of her kind," Big Al said.

"I don't see her, it, ah, whatever." Tommy couldn't see the stuffed beast anywhere.

"Oh dear. Looks like she may have slipped away." Big Al took a few steps behind the counter to get a better look at the entranceway.

Tommy's eyes were as big as saucers. *How could a stuffed animal slip away? What was this guy talking about?*

"You did well today, Thomas. It took courage to defend your friend like that. But I'm afraid Jimmy Wayne is gunning for you now. You laid him out pretty good." Big Al remarked. "Lilly respects courage and loyalty."

Tommy slumped back on the stool. He fidgeted with a napkin still there. "What am I gonna do? I'm afraid. But I can't let him hurt her. I'll kill him first. I don't care what happens to me."

"What if he doesn't return to school?" Big Al asked.

"That would be great. Wait, what are you saying?" Tommy felt queasy in his stomach. He'd hoped to never see Jimmy Wayne again, but not in the way he perceived Big Al's question.

Big Al smiled, "Would you like another?"

"Vanilla Fizz? Oh, ah, no. No, thank you. What do you mean? If he doesn't return to school?" Tommy couldn't let Big Al's question go.

"What if, who doesn't return to school?" Phyliss had come out of the bathroom unnoticed. Your, your eye," she said to Big Al. His left eye no longer had the second iris and pupil; it was normal like the right.

Big Al didn't respond. He simply tilted his head as if he didn't know what she was saying. But Tommy noticed the corners of his mouth turn up, and he knew Big Al understood.

"Wouldn't your life be easier if Jimmy wasn't there? Wouldn't both of your lives be easier?" Big Al asked.

"Yeah, but…I don't want him murdered." Phyliss stated.

"Who said anything about murder?" Big Al snapped. "I just gave you soda and ice cream. What type of individual do you think I am?"

"I'm sorry, mister. I didn't mean anything by it. I just thought you were, you know, saying…" Phyliss stammered.

"Saying what, young miss?" Big Al paused. "Well, I'm afraid it isn't up to me anyway. It looks as if Lilly may have decided to take things into her own…um…paws." Big Al chuckled.

"Lilly?" Phyliss didn't understand initially, but a spark went off in her head. She turned to see the same thing Tommy had noticed: the Poliger wasn't standing beside the door. "YOU MEAN THAT THING IS REAL?"

"What is real? You saw her when you first came in, didn't you? You touched her? What else do you need to convince yourself of the world around you?" Big Al said.

"Yeah, but that was a stuffed animal. Not alive." Phyliss responded.

Big Al let out a chuckle. "You have a lot to learn. Anyway, as I said to young Thomas here, she seems to have taken a liking to you both. Otherwise, you're touching her leg, well…" Big Al was interrupted by a loud roar coming from outside. They all turned toward the front.

Tommy and Phyliss followed Big Al to the large window beside the entrance door. Big Al sighed, "I'm afraid she may have decided to take the law into her own hands."

"Law? What law?" Tommy asked.

"Natural law. The only one she follows." Big Al responded.

"Are you saying she's going to kill Jimmy?" Phyliss's heart was thumping. Yes, she was angry. Yes, she hoped to never see Jimmy Wayne again, but she did not wish him death. "Please, mister, Big Al, you have to stop her. Please." She begged.

"I'm not sure I can." Big Al said.

"You have to!" Phyliss pleaded.

Big Al looked her square in the eye. "Even after he hurt you?"

"Yes." She responded without hesitation.

Big Al looked at Tommy, "And you? You know, he could have you arrested for assault with a deadly weapon."

Tommy nodded, "I don't care. It wouldn't be right." Big Al could see the sincerity in both their eyes. Another roar and a loud crash drew their attention outside. When they looked at Big Al, his clothes had changed. He was wearing the same apparel they first saw on the porch.

"You both have worked up quite a tab today. You owe me. Don't forget it." Big Al tipped the wide-brim hat before going outside.

The sky darkened, and the wind howled. Dust and debris filled the air, and they struggled to see. A quick movement of orange and white flashed. Then another roar, and a third. "That must be Lilly. But that other sound wasn't the same as hers," Tommy remarked.

Then, as quickly as the stormy weather came through, the atmosphere suddenly calmed. The wind slowed, and the outside began to lighten. Phyliss felt a pinch on her leg. The gray cat's claws drew her attention. "What is it, girl? Do you want us to follow you?"

Stormy began to walk toward the bathroom, and Phyliss and Tommy followed. The cat led them down the dark hall and sat beside a door. She looked at the door and then at the two of them before meowing.

Tommy pushed, and the door swung open. Both had to cover their eyes from the sun. It was bright outside again, as it was when they entered the Emporium. The air was calm and clear. The door shut behind them, and they realized they were at the rear of the store. Their bikes were lying on the grass in front of them.

Tommy and Phyliss picked up their bikes and walked them to the front. The Emporium's neon sign was no longer lit. "LOOK!" Phyliss yelled, pointing into the park.

Tommy and Phyliss jumped on their bikes and pedaled as fast as possible. A semi-tractor trailer had smashed Jimmy's Gremlin into a big Oak Tree on the park's edge. The big rig came to a stop across the road.

They watched as an ambulance rushed to the scene. Paramedics and the Jenks Twp. Volunteer Fire Department extracted Jimmy and his friends from the car. A Forest County Deputy Sheriff directed traffic while his partner talked to witnesses.

Tommy rode up to the deputy, "Are they going to be alright?"

"Did you see the crash, son?" The deputy asked.

"No, sir. But I heard it." Tommy answered.

"They're going to be fine. The driver suffered a broken nose and some minor head injury. Probably has a concussion. That's what happens when you fail to stop at this intersection. They're lucky they weren't killed. Fortunately, the truck driver wasn't going that fast. I'd say they'll be in the hospital for a few days, maybe a couple of months. Best ride along now." The deputy stated.

Tommy returned to Phyliss, who was still seated on her bike at the end of the park. "Are they okay?" she asked.

"Yeah, banged up. They think the crash broke Jimmy's nose." Tommy said.

"I guess that's good luck for you," Phyliss remarked.

"Yeah, I suppo…" Tommy stopped midway through his response. Phyliss turned to see what he was looking at. Big Al's Emporium was gone. The two friends pedaled to the vacant lot and stopped. There were two indentations where their bikes had been. And their tire tracks showed in the tall grass, too. But there was no Emporium, no building, nothing but tall weeds.

Tommy and Phyliss looked at each other with puzzlement. They both turned to the intersection as the ambulance was driving away. They looked back at the vacant lot one more time as they pedaled out of town. Neither said a word nor spoke of this day ever again.

Find out what happens to mi Lady, the Carriage Driver, and Colonel Volker in Book two of *A Cry in the Moon's Light, The Undead Wars!*

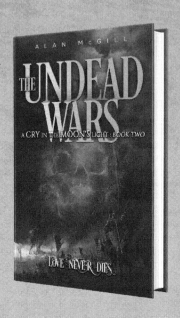

★★★★★

HARROWING YET COMPELLING...A MUST-READ GOTHIC HORROR/DARK FANTASY NOVEL!

The perfect sequel to A Cry in the Moon's Light expands upon the mythos and world-building of the first novel, allowing readers to dive deeper into the world the author has crafted. The author's dark and grim imagery in the book is spine-chilling and beautiful in its delivery. The story's fantastic character development and pacing became the heart of the narrative. The pacing matched the suddenness and shock of the emerging threat of this undead army, especially the emergence of Alessandra as the heroine who has to bring these ragtag fighters together to face this undead threat was great to see come to life on the page.

GO AHEAD, DON'T BE AFRAID,
IT'S THE LAST ONE...FOR NOW.

THE GRINNING MAN

INDRID COLD

Tall timber was one of the reasons John built his camp on the plot next to Casey's Corner. He'd been friends with the owner for many years, so when it was available to purchase, he jumped on the chance.

The little building sat on the edge of the Allegheny National Forest amongst a row of camps. These were all situated near some of the most densely wooded areas in western Pennsylvania. The tree's canopy was high above the ground, leaving the ground below free of vegetation. This uninhibited view created great hunting opportunities in The Keystone State.

The Marienville area had a limited population, which made deer and other game plentiful. It wasn't unusual to see herds of 20 or 30 deer in those woods.

John and his family were avid sportsmen. Each year, he and his two brothers would take his only son hunting on the first day of buck. They would walk miles into the deepest part of the woods in search of trophy deer. Nearly every member of the hunting camp got one on the first day. They'd return later to hang and butcher their harvest.

John and his wife Nancy awoke before the sun came up. John started a pot of coffee while she cooked breakfast. John was pleased when he looked out the window. "We got a good bit of snow. Must be four inches. We haven't had this much snow in a few years. I got a good feeling."

Nancy placed a couple of eggs and toast in front of him. "Should I wake the boys?"

"Nah. Let 'em sleep." He responded. "They'll be up soon. Phil is going with Bob today; he can go with me tomorrow. I want to get going before everyone wakes up."

John always got up earlier than everyone else. He preferred to hike to his favorite spot without revealing to anyone where it was. Sportsmen can be like that. Once they find a honey hole, they keep it to themselves; otherwise, it will be overrun by hunters. John had bagged some impressive bucks at that place over the years. In fact, two of them had been featured in the Pennsylvania Game News Magazine.

"Here, good luck today. Be careful." Nancy gave him a lunch bag and a thermos of coffee, then kissed his cheek before he went out the door.

It was four a.m. when he crossed the road to walk the old logging trail. John passed quietly by his friend Mark's camp next to the trail. Everyone there was still sleeping, but this camp wasn't as dedicated as his. He'd see them later tonight at the bonfire.

John trudged three miles over small hills and two streams until he reached the split oak. Many years ago, lightning struck the tree, and half its trunk fell across the road, blocking the way. The other half still lived, sprouting new leaves each year. This was the marker John used to turn southeast to reach his secret spot.

Before he left the logging trail, John cut the limb off an eastern hemlock. As he hiked across the unmarked wooded area, John swept the pine branch over the snow to hide his tracks.

After he reached a small mound several hundred feet away, John ditched the pine branch and continued over the ridge. A mile or so later, he reached the edge of his prime hunting ground. This was an open area of tall grass. The tree line stopped as the hill sloped down into this valley. Giant boulders lined the forest edge, shielding the view of the open field. It was as if they were placed there to guard this sacred spot. And it was home to some of the biggest deer anywhere in the forest.

It was still dark, and it would be a couple of hours before hunting season officially began. John pulled the rifle to his shoulder to look through the scope at the valley below. It was too dark to see anything, but he knew there were deer, and he had a good feeling. But that was all about to change.

He crept his way to a place he liked to set up between two large rocks. This was one of many, but it was his favorite as it provided the best view of the field. John brushed snow off a flat rock nestled beside a larger one that he often used as a seat. John sat and poured himself a cup of coffee to wait for the dawn.

He could see the steam coming off the cup as his eyes drifted to the heavens. The air was cold, and the sky was filled with so many stars he could not even begin to count them. As he admired the night sky, he noticed three bright lights far off in the distance. *That's a weird-looking group of stars,* he thought.

He noticed movement in the valley below as he took another sip of coffee. Even without the scope, he could tell it was a monster buck. He slowly put the cup down on the rock beside him, laid the rifle across, and lined up the movement within the scope.

He couldn't believe his eyes. Although his eyes strained in the darkness, it was one of the biggest bucks he'd ever seen. The animal had snuck through the rocks, and when its silhouette stood against the snowy background, he could tell it was huge. The outline of the rack revealed it was non-typical. He estimated the weight to be in excess of two hundred pounds. His breathing increased when he estimated the scoring might rival Edward Knox's record set in 1942. Nobody had ever taken a buck this big in Forest County.

Although it wasn't legal to shoot yet, he flipped the switch on his safety and prepared to fire. This was a once-in-a-lifetime buck, and John wouldn't let this opportunity slip away. And he was so far back in the woods that nobody was even close to him. The odds of getting caught were slim to none.

The meaty part of his index finger now touched the trigger. His breathing slowed as his mind focused. He could see the buck's giant rack and used that as a starting point. He lowered the crosshairs over the dark shape in position to hit the chest.

John began to squeeze when the entire sky lit! Three beams of light shined over the field. One landed on the big buck. He was right. This deer was enormous. John instinctively looked up, but he was forced to use a hand to shield his eyes. The light was so bright he couldn't see what the object was.

John averted his eyes down the valley to see the big buck running across the field at full speed. The deer was beyond the light when everything suddenly went dark. John looked at the sky, but it was empty. Whatever illuminated this field was gone!

John stood, his hands shaking. *What the hell was that?* His thoughts turned to his wife. *Nancy isn't going to believe this one.*

Nancy was not someone who entertained the idea of UFOs or such things. She was a devout Catholic who saw stories like those as the work of the devil.

The others at the camp weren't going to believe him either. John began to doubt himself. *Did I imagine this?* John tried to shrug it off, but the deer nagged at him. He was perfectly willing to dismiss the strange lights. Maybe it was some type of meteor or something. But a trophy buck like that comes once in a lifetime.

John hoisted the rifle over his shoulder and grabbed his flashlight. Hunting season was officially starting at 7:20 a.m., but according to his watch, it was only 5:30 a.m. He had plenty of time to sneak down there quietly and look for any signs of that buck.

John reached the area where the deer had been. The flashlight lit up the tracks, showing that it had come down the big hill to his left. He followed the tracks to a spot void of snow. *This must have been where he stood, but why is there no snow here?* He mused.

The question was quickly replaced by a sick feeling. If he hadn't imagined or dreamed of this deer, *does this mean the lights were real?*

Then, his flashlight revealed a twinkle in the center of the snow-less area. He placed the beam squarely on the object. It was a round sphere sitting atop the grass less than twenty feet away. John cautiously walked to it. The grass was pressed flat in a weird pattern. "What the hell is that?"

John looked around nervously. He shined the light 360 degrees to make sure nobody was around. Then he heard something move. Instinctively, he shined the light at the sound. The sphere had rolled toward him. The orb gave a twinkle when the light hit it.

The movement freaked John out, but the closer the object got, the calmer he became. It rolled slowly to his feet. Now he could see the surface wasn't completely smooth. There were rough patches and smooth places in between. It reminded him of a globe of the earth. The smooth, shiny places would be the oceans, and the rough spots would be the continents. However, it wasn't the Earth or any planet he'd ever seen.

John knelt beside the object, no longer afraid or apprehensive. He reached under to cradle the orb in his hands. The feeling of calm turned into a pleasant sensation as he stood. The object was solid and felt strong—neither light nor heavy.

John raised it to his chest, and when it was closer to his face, he could see his smile in the reflection. His eyes twinkled like the stars reflected in the sphere. But his expression changed when he noticed three bright lights appear there, too.

John's head swung around to see the same bright lights were back in the sky, and they were getting bigger. He tucked the sphere under his arm and raced up the hill. The elation he'd felt turned to fear.

John didn't stop for his thermos, lunch, or anything else, he just kept running. He kept turning his head to watch the lights. They kept getting bigger as if they were chasing him.

John was no longer a young man, and running in the cold weather was especially hard. The brisk air filled his lungs, and he began to slow. His legs ached, and there was a pinch in his chest. John's father died of a heart attack, and he knew the signs.

He stopped behind a tree to recuperate. He reached into his pocket for his cell phone. It was dead. *The cold must have drained the battery.* He peaked around the tree, and his heart nearly stopped.

Hovering above was a large triangular craft. It wasn't right over him, but close enough that he should have been able to hear something, yet the ship made no sound. There were three lights on each point of the triangle, too. They weren't as intense as before, but enough to light up the forest below.

John set the silver globe on the ground and slowly pulled the rifle to his shoulder. He used the scope to get a better look at the craft. It was flat-sided and made of some type of black metal. The surface was smooth, and there was a row of windows that went all the way around.

Behind the windows, he could see three men walking inside the craft. They wore dark, iridescent clothing and slicked-back weird-looking hair. Then he noticed one of the men staring right at him!

He appeared like any ordinary man except for the permanent smile etched across his face. John was so startled he ducked behind the tree again. His heart really pumped now, and his breathing increased.

"AHHHH!" John screamed. The same man from the craft was now standing less than 10 feet away on the forest floor!

"My people call me Indrid Cold. What are you called?" The man's mouth did not move, yet somehow John heard this, not with his ears, but with his mind.

John's mouth opened, but he couldn't speak. Confused and afraid, images of his life ran through his mind. The first was his wife, Nancy, then their home in Rural Valley, and finally, his mailbox with their name painted on the side.

"There is no need to be afraid, John Lipinski. We mean you no harm. We have only come for the sphere." The Grinning Man did not move his mouth, yet John heard this, too.

John didn't realize when he fell, he'd instinctively let go of his rifle to grab the orb. The very object he now clutched to his chest and the one thing this being wanted.

His fear was overwhelming. The being calling himself Indrid Cold took a step toward him. Without giving it a thought, John was running. He ran through the snow, down the other side of the hill, as fast as he could.

He kept peeking over his shoulder, but the being was not chasing. The hill blocked the view of the spacecraft, but the ambient light on the other side remained. The unidentified flying object was not following.

When John turned to face the direction, he was running, a shack appeared out of nowhere. It was sitting right beside the split oak tree, and John stopped. The odd little shop had a big neon sign that read, Emporium. A smaller sign in the front window said Open. *Where'd that come from?* He thought.

John went to the door and opened it. He rushed inside and closed the door, still grasping the silver orb. A bell hanging above the door rang once when the door opened and once when it closed.

"WHOA!" John screamed at the sight of the giant Poliger looming at him. "What the hell is that thing?" John looked out the front window nervously, still pressing his back to the door.

"AHH," he gasped at the sound of Big Al's voice. "You alright friend?"

"Who the hell are you?" John asked.

Big Al stood behind a counter beyond the Poliger. He used a rag to clean some objects he'd removed from a display case. "Most folks call me Big Al."

"Are you some kind of…alien?" John asked nervously.

Big Al laughed. "Why on earth would you ask that?"

John took another quick look out the front window. He couldn't see much because it was dark, but nothing seemed to be chasing him, and there weren't any strange lights. He stood up straight and stepped from the door.

Big Al extended an inviting hand toward a stool in front of the counter. "Come, sit. Let me get you some tea or something to calm you?" But John shook his head no.

"I usually don't open this early, friend. I like to use this time for some much-needed cleaning. I guess the open sign in the window might be a bit confusing." Big Al walked to the neon sign and pulled a chain, which turned the sign off.

"How are you, or rather, what are you doing here? I mean, this is the middle of nowhere. I've been coming to these woods for 40 years, and I've never seen any kind of store out here. Why would anyone build one in the middle of the forest?" Then John's nervousness worsened, "Or…are you with them?"

"Who?" Big Al chuckled. "There's nobody else here, friend."

"I was hunting a mile or so down the valley." John started.

"Yes, of course, it's the first day of buck season. There are lots of big deer out here," Big Al commented.

"You're going to think I'm crazy." John looked around and then became distracted by all the weird stuff he saw. "What kind of damned store is this anyway?"

"I assure you; I will not think you are crazy. Many things are possible in the Emporium. As you say, why put a store way out in the middle of the forest? We're used to strange things here, aren't we Lilly?" Big Al patted the giant taxidermy beast on the side.

John's eyes went over the store a little closer this time. It was filled with usual things, many of which he recognized and plenty he did not, such as the giant beast Big Al stood next to.

"You seem out of breath. Were you being chased by something, maybe someone?" Big Al returned behind the counter. A warm smile came across his face, an assuring gesture to provide a feeling of calm. He extended his hand once again, inviting John to sit on the stool in front of him.

John's breathing slowed as he began to relax. He took a seat on the stool as Big Al continued to wipe the round stones from the case. "What are those?" John asked.

"These? Black polymetallic sea nodules. They are rich with nickel, manganese, and cobalt." John looked perplexed, so Big Al continued, "They produced something called Dark Oxygen."

John jumped off the stool and took a few steps back. Big Al lifted his palm. "Easy, friend. That's just a term used to describe how they create oxygen without photosynthesis. These were found on the ocean's floor at a depth void of light. Perfectly safe. In fact, the oxygen produced by these minerals is very therapeutic. I thought their effects might calm you. That's why I invited you to sit closer while I cleared the dust off them."

John sat back on the stool skeptically before continuing with his story. "As I said, I was hunting. A huge buck in the fie…" John stopped himself. He didn't want to reveal too much information about his favorite spot. "Anyway. I saw this buck, and then some strange lights from the sky scared it away." John paused, looking for any sign of skepticism from Big Al, but there was none.

"Go on. You were out at the big boulder field to the east of here when the lights scared away your prized buck." Big Al saw John's reaction. "Don't worry, friend. I don't hunt, not deer anyway."

John's head turned at all the taxidermy hanging from the walls. Big Al laughed, "I didn't kill them. These trophies were barters." Big Al leaned on the counter, "I didn't tell anyone where to find them either." Big Al paused to look John in the eyes, "I've known about Big

Boulder Field for many years. You're the only one who hunts there. Your secret is safe with me."

"You know, you still didn't answer why anyone in their right mind would build a store in the middle of the forest. And, come to think of it, there's no electricity out here. How are these lights working?" John asked.

Big Al leaned back and picked up another nodule. "Did you come in here so I could explain my business plan? Or do you want to finish telling me what happened?"

John shrugged, "As I was saying, these three bright lights scared away the buck. They scared me, too, so I ran up the hill. Then I saw a big, I dunno…"

"You left out a step, didn't you?" Big Al asked.

John instinctively clutched the globe closer to his chest.

"Yes, exactly. That's what I'm talking about. Where did you get that?" Big Al pointed softly at the silver orb.

John looked down, squeezing it tighter. "I found it where the deer had been. The lights in the sky started coming at me, so I picked it up and ran."

Big AL continued to wipe the nodules, "Okay, so you got over the hill, then saw a big what?"

"Some type of…spaceship." John's eyes lowered.

"Spaceship?" Big Al responded.

"You see, that's what I'm talking about. People are going to think I'm crazy." John objected.

"Hold on, friend. I don't think you're crazy. I'm just making sure I understood you correctly. Why do you think it was a spaceship? Did you see it come from space? So far, all I heard was a triangular-shaped aircraft scared away the buck and then came after you." Big Al tried to reassure him.

That queasy feeling returned. "I never said it was a triangle? How'd you know that?"

"You said three lights. Triangles have three sides; hence the first three letters, T R I." Big Al responded.

John realized much of what this guy was suggesting would explain many things. He saw the craft in the sky, but he didn't know where it came from. Maybe it was some type of airplane? But that didn't explain the creepy guy with the permanent smile.

"There was this guy that came from the…craft. His hair was slicked back, and he was dressed in dark clothes. He had this creepy…"

Big Al cut him off, "Grin. Constant smile?"

"YES." John blurted.

"Let me guess. He said his name was Indrid Cold. Scratch that. He said he was called Indrid Cold." Big Al scoffed.

"YES. That's exactly what he said. So, he's real?" John asked.

"What do you mean by real?" Big Al asked.

"He's a man? Or is he some type of alien?" John's mind raced.

Big Al was about to answer John's question when he noticed a strange glow coming from the front window. Big Al stopped what he was doing and went to look out. John followed, still holding the orb.

A few hundred yards away, near the hilltop, spotlights searched the woods. There were three beams of light emanating from above the trees and bouncing all around. "What do you suppose that is?" Big Al asked.

John took a few steps away from the window. "That's them. That's what I was telling you about."

"Well, I'd say they really want that orb. You're perfectly safe here, but you can't stay in the Emporium forever, I'm afraid. And you're quite a few miles from your cabin." Big Al continued to watch the lights moving over the forest floor. "And they're coming this way."

"What am I gonna do?" John asked, sweat coming off his brow.

"Let me go outside and see what they want. You stay inside." Big Al said, turning the doorknob.

The bell above the door chimed. Big Al went outside and shut the door behind him. John moved to the window and peeked out. The grinning man stood in the woods a hundred feet from the logging road. Big Al walked off the Emporium's porch and stood facing him.

John set the orb beside the Poliger, then he opened the door and stepped outside the shop. His eyes bulged when he saw the sky. It was still dark and full of stars, but now there were two planets filling the horizon. One was large, like Jupiter. The smaller one was just behind it as if peeking around the bigger one.

As he stared at them, John realized they weren't planets but eyeballs! These were two iris' each with a pupil. They both faced the ground and moved as if watching Big Al and the Grinning Man.

WHAT THE HELL? WHERE AM I? These loud thoughts echoed in John's mind. He could feel his sanity slipping away, and then he heard Big Al's voice.

"WHAT IS IT YOU WANT?" Big Al yelled to The Grinning Man.

The Grinning Man's lips did not move. He stared at Big Al for a few moments, then pointed at John who was standing on the Emporium's porch behind Big Al.

Big Al didn't flinch. He continued to look at The Grinning Man before responding.

"HE NO LONGER HAS THE ORB." Big Al stated.

Again, The Grinning Man communicated without moving his lips. As he did, the wind increased. It picked up loose snow and created a deafening howl as it careened through the trees.

Big Al was forced to lift his voice above the swirling wind. "I DON'T CARE WHAT YOU WISH FOR THE INHABITANTS. YOU NEED TO LEAVE, OR I ASSURE YOU, YOU WILL UNDERSTAND OF WHAT I AM CAPABLE." Big Al yelled his response at The Grinning Man before turning to John, "Go back inside John…NOW."

John didn't hesitate. He rushed back in and slammed the door. The entire scene was surreal. The backdrop sky of two eyeballs watching the forest, Big Al squaring off against this weird Smiling Man, a flying saucer, er, triangle high overhead, and the sudden gust of weather.

Big Al held onto his hat as he accepted one final thought from the being known as Indrid Cold. Begrudgingly, he returned to the Emporium. He found John squatting beside the Poliger, trying to pick up the orb, only now, it was too heavy.

Big Al wiped the snow from his arms, then slapped his hat against his leg to remove what had accumulated. Then he looked at John, who was still tirelessly trying to pick up the orb. "Perhaps you should give them the item?"

John responded between grunts and groans, "But it chose me."

"What do you mean, it chose you?" Big Al asked.

"When I saw it in the field, it rolled toward me. I stopped, and it rolled right up to my leg. I picked it up and…"

"Yes, what?" Big Al asked.

John finally managed to lift the sphere. "It was like it wanted me to help it get away." He was out of breath, huffing and puffing as he held the object. "I don't understand. It wasn't that heavy before."

"Perhaps it no longer requires your assistance." Big Al suggested.

John became twitchy, "I don't want you to sell it."

"Not to worry. Nothing is for sale here." Big Al responded.

"Not for sale? What do you mean? Isn't this an antique store?" John asked.

Big Al smiled, "Do the things in this place really seem like antiques to you?" Big Al wasn't expecting a response, "It will be safe with me. Worry not; nothing will happen here. The Emporium is protected by the Time Cosmic."

John's attention was suddenly drawn to the window. The winter weather had died down, and he could see The Grinning Man on the road in front of the Emporium. Now that he was so close, John saw him much more clearly, the permanent smile still etched on his face.

John was so creeped out by The Grinning Man's smile that he nodded his agreement to Big Al. John took a few steps and then placed the sphere on the counter. As John kept the orb from rolling away, Big Al ran to the back of the store. He grabbed a strange garment off a pair of blue Elk antlers, then rushed to the orb and covered it with the cloak.

The cloak appeared to be made of dragon scales. If there was such a thing. *What is this thing made of?* John reached to touch one of the panels when Big Al snapped, "Do not remove the cloak!"

John yanked back his hand. He watched from the front window as Big Al went outside and stepped onto the logging trail to face Indrid Cold. This time, the two were twenty feet apart: Big Al on one side and Cold on the other.

John didn't know if Indrid Cold was communicating as the being stood motionless with the same permanent smile. The only voice John could hear was Big Al's. "This place is under my protection, Lanulosian, or whatever you claim to be. Go bother Point Pleasant or some other place."

The wind started to howl, hurling snow through the trees. John could barely see Big Al now, nor Indrid Cold. The front door bounced as gusts of wind slammed against it. John's curiosity got the best of him, and he opened the door. The wind was so strong that he nearly dislocated his shoulder when it caught the door. He struggled with both hands to pull it shut. Once it latched, a heavy gust tossed him off the porch.

John managed to crawl behind a large tree. The wind swirled all around, but the giant trunk prevented him from receiving the brunt of it. This allowed him to stand, although he continued to be pelted by snow and flying debris.

The sky was pitch black, but he could no longer see the giant eyeballs peering down. Hugging the tree, he peeked around it. Out of nowhere, Big Al was suddenly nose-to-nose with him. "AH," he screamed.

Big Al's eyes glowed, and John saw that his left eye had two irises, just like the sky! One was blue, the other yellow. Big Al grabbed John's head and pulled him close. He could feel the hot breath on his ear as Big Al spoke, "The orb will be safe in the Emporium. Go back to your life. Go back to your wife. Take her to breakfast and cherish what you have. Speak not of this ever again."

Then, all at once, it was over. John could not feel the grip of Big Al's hand on his neck. The wind was gone. The sky was normal. There were no planets or eyeballs; they were just the stars above the coming dawn. Big Al was gone.

John was able to stand without any resistance. He took a few steps around the big tree, and there was nothing. The Emporium wasn't there. Ten feet away, he saw the thermos of coffee, his lunch bag, and his rifle lying in the middle of the old logging road.

John gathered his belongings and then checked his rifle. The safety was on, and there was a round in the chamber. His head snapped in every direction; the woods were normal.

Ahead, John heard rustling behind the split oak tree. Then he spotted movement on the other side, going from left to right. John pulled the rifle to his shoulder and flipped off the safety. If The Grinning Man, this Big Al character, or anyone else wanted to find out, he was ready.

A bead of sweat rolled down his temple onto his cheek. He followed the movement of shadow with his scope. One, two, three, HOLD. He moved his finger off the trigger. It was…that big assed buck! The same non-traditional buck he saw in the middle of the boulder field.

The deer looked right at him. Its nostrils flared as it expelled cold air. The buck continued to stare at him as sunlight peeked through the trees. A gunshot rang out in the distance. Then another. The official start of antler season was underway.

The big buck never flinched. It continued to stare at John, waiting. John removed his finger from the trigger well and flipped the safety back on. He lowered the rifle, then slung it over his shoulder. The buck stomped its hoof, snorted, then trotted off.

John slowly walked the three miles back to camp. As he approached the crossing of Route 899, John looked at his watch. *5:30? Must be broken.* He reached into his pocket and pulled out the cellphone. Much to his surprise, the phone came on. The time was 8:30. He looked back at his watch, which now read 8:30.

Nancy was sitting in the living room reading a book when he came through the door. "John? What's wrong? Are you okay?"

"Yeah, I'm fine." John put his rifle, thermos, and lunch bag in the kitchen, then sat on the sofa.

"You're never back this early. What happened?" Nancy was a little concerned. She had never known John not to be excited during deer season. He'd left with high hopes today. The snow made it easier to see, and the day was clear.

"Nothin. I went out to my usual spot, was having a cup of coffee, and saw…" John looked at his wife with a loving heart. "What are you reading?"

Nancy lifted the cover, "Um, Bumper City. It's a detective thriller set in the future. The author is a local of sorts. I guess his grandfather built a camp around here years ago. Alan McGill. I read his werewolf story and really liked it. I thought I'd give this a shot."

"Is it any good?" John asked.

"Yeah. So far. I'm only onto the second chapter." She responded.

"I thought you didn't like science fiction?" John asked.

"I don't, but this isn't that bad. There's a talking car; he's actually the best character." Nancy smiled warmly at her husband, "Now, why are you back so soon? You were saying you saw something?"

"Huh? Oh, yeah. I saw the biggest deer of my life." John answered.

"So, where is it?" Nancy asked.

"I missed," John said.

"You missed. John Henry Lipinski, you mean to tell me you finally missed a shot?" Nancy laughed.

"Nobody's perfect, I guess. Did you eat breakfast yet?" He asked.

"I never eat. I made the boys breakfast and sat down." She responded.

"Let's go into town and have breakfast at the 66 Diner," John said.

"You're not going back out?" Nancy asked.

"I think I've had all the excitement I can handle for one season." John chuckled. "Besides, you've been cooking me breakfast here for years. I think it's time someone cooked yours. I can't cook worth a damn, but I can certainly take you out."

John and Nancy drove into Marienville and ate breakfast that morning. Nancy was happy to spend some quiet time with her husband. John was happy to forget what had happened earlier.

John would not be bothered by Indrid Cold again, but it was not the last time we'd hear of The Grinning Man.

TO BE CONTINUED...

Last but certainly not least, the exciting prequel to *A Cry in the Moon's Light*. Travel with Alessandra and Seth as they fall in love. And see how William becomes so twisted and evil, then transforming into the Black Wolf!

★★★★★

LOVED THIS BOOK!

LOVED this book! Had a blast reading this! There aren't too many books that have horror, romance, and history elements in one and that's what makes this book so unique. Such a spooky read! - Brit

★★★★★

OMG! A BEAUTIFUL PIECE OF ART THAT HAPPENS TO BE A HORROR STORY

WOW, it's a quick read, but one of the most enjoyable books I have read in a long time. A mixture of fictional history, romance, and horror! Warning you may be up at night after reading, thinking about the heroes and creatures that inhabit Mr. McGill's mind.

MORE FROM THE AUTHOR

Marienville has always been a special place to me. My grandfather built a camp off Route 899 right across from the infamous *Casey's Corner*. I spent much of my youth hunting, hiking, sitting around the campfire, and other activities there. So, it was no accident that I decided the setting for these stories as the gateway to the Allegheny National Forest.

To this day, I drive through the area, and it was not long ago the first story, *Penny for your Thoughts,* came to mind. I had stopped at the Kwik-Fill convenience store across from SCI Forest County State Prison. (Yes, both places are real.) It was a hot day with a small breeze. As I pumped gas, I noticed how quiet it was with little traffic or people. I began to wonder, what it would be like if a stranger were to pass through and find himself completely alone?

I had to find a central character, and thus Big Al. This was inspired by a nickname bestowed upon me by a friend at work. After some successes, he began to refer to me as *Big Al the Dream Maker*. While I am nothing like our shopkeeper, Big Al, I thought it was a fun concept and enjoyed bringing that character to life within these pages. Humble beginnings you might say.

I trust you enjoyed these quick tales of, I don't know, what would you call them? Terror, Supernatural Suspense, or maybe just weird. Hopefully you found them as fun to read as they were to write.

Look for more of these short story books of Big Al the Dream Maker. Who knows where they will take place, or what Big Al will be managing. It could be the Emporium, perhaps a library, but wherever he turns up, I am sure it will be…curious, odd, and strange.

Until next time, be kind and take care of one another.
—Alan

FOLLOW ME

ALANMCGILL14

 @AlanMcGill14

Following helps promote the books.

ALAN MCGILL'S AUDIOBOOKS

If you are a fan of audiobooks, I narrate and produce all my own. They can be found anywhere audiobooks are found or you can find links on my website.

ALANMCGILLBOOKS.COM

Scan this QR code for more

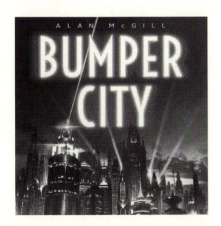

AWESOME ADVENTURE!
What an exciting and futuristic story! I loved the twists and turns of *Bumper City* with its dark underbelly of crime and suspense.

A CRY IN THE MOON'S LIGHT AUDIOBOOKS!

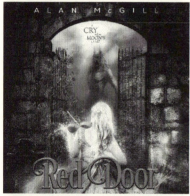

BREATHTAKING AND ATMOSPHERIC!

If you were to combine the original terror of Hollywood's Universal Monster flicks with the storytelling found in classic radio shows and infuse it with a dramatic Gothic and dark fairy tale story, author Alan McGill's "A Cry in the Moon's Light" would be the story you heard.

The author's audiobook release is an instant hit, with dynamic vocal work to bring both the narration and characters to life perfectly. The buildup of tension and atmosphere using expert sound effects and music really made this feel like a cinematic quality story and a gripping dark fantasy world that you can easily get lost in.

Don't worry, this book will be coming on audiobook soon too!

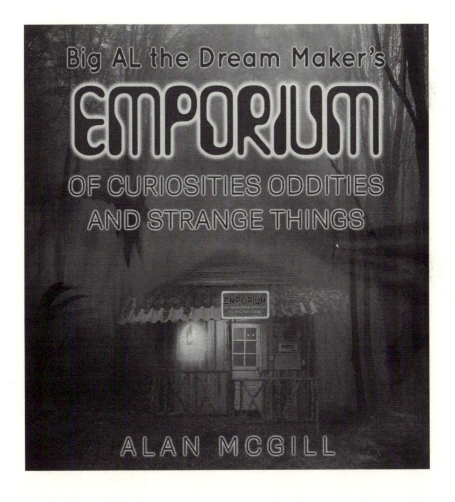

HEY...YOU
LEAVE A REVIEW

Reviews matter.
We all try, but they're hard to come by
They mean the world to me, if they come by thee

Amazon
Goodreads
Barnes & Noble
Book Bub
Books a Million BAM
Audible
Spotify

Anywhere you find my work!

THANK YOU
TO ALL WHO TOOK
THE TIME TO
LEAVE A REVIEW

What on earth is this?
A place to make a list.
Your thoughts
your dreams
your plots

I do hope you enjoyed my little stories within, so much so, it made you grin.
Look for the Emporium in other parts of Pennsylvania
Volumes 1, 2 & 3, of madness and mania

If you found words that weren't quite right
Or things that gave you fright
Place them here
Without any fear

_____
_____
_____
_____
_____
_____
_____
_____
_____
_____

I WANT TO THANK THE TEAM

Cover design by Emily of Emily's World of Design

Interior Art by Johnny Haxby

Formatting/Interior Design by Liz Schreiter

You make these books special!

UNTIL NEXT TIME...
I'll tell Stormy to unlock the door!

I got nothing left. That's all.
Leave a review!

Made in the USA
Columbia, SC
15 November 2024